**Tasha turned** [...]
**her finger.**

'Real gold,' she sa[...]
really my husband. [...] strange.'

Chase took her hand in his for a moment, his
thumb stroking the ring on her finger. 'The fact
that you are wearing that piece of metal on your
finger doesn't mean I have any rights over you.'

'Legally you do,' said Tash.

He smiled and that unsettling look was back in
his warm, dark eyes. 'I could kiss you...'

**Linda Miles** was born in Kenya, spent her childhood in Argentina, Brazil and Peru, and completed her education in England. She is a keen rider, and wrote her first story at the age of ten when laid up with a broken leg after a fall. She considers three months a year the minimum acceptable holiday allowance but has never got an employer to see reason, and took up writing romances as a way to have adventures and see the world.

**Recent titles by the same author:**

HIS GIRL MONDAY TO FRIDAY

# LAST-MINUTE
# BRIDEGROOM

BY
LINDA MILES

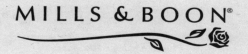

MILLS & BOON and MILLS & BOON with the Rose Device are registered trademarks of the publisher.

First published in Great Britain 1999
Harlequin Mills & Boon Limited,
Eton House, 18-24 Paradise Road, Richmond, Surrey TW9 1SR

© Linda Miles 1999

ISBN 0 263 81754 7

Set in Times Roman 10½ on 11½ pt.
02-9908-55808 C1

Printed and bound in Spain
by Litografía Rosés, S.A., Barcelona

# CHAPTER ONE

RAIN poured from a pitch-black sky. The wind howled through the woods. Not the best night for a two-mile walk up a bad country road, but at this point Natasha Merrill didn't have much choice. The nearest taxi service was thirty miles away; she'd called the house, but there had been no reply.

Not for the first time she had glared from the station phone booth to the house at the top of the hill. All the lights were lit; her father was home, but the phone rang ten, twenty, thirty times and went unanswered. Her father was obviously in his study. The phone could not be heard from his study. Well-meaning people who did not know him well sometimes pointed out that he could easily put an extension through to the study.

'I *could*,' was the usual reply. 'But in that case I would have to find some other room for my study where I would not be disturbed by the phone.'

Tasha sighed. She'd been trying desperately to call him all day, but now, perversely, she was almost glad she hadn't been able to reach him. She didn't *want* to tell him about it on the phone. She wanted to throw herself in his arms and cry until she couldn't cry any more. There wouldn't be anything he could do, but it wouldn't matter. He would hold her, and talk about what had happened, and after a while it would remind him of something completely irrelevant but more interesting to a professor of philosophy. He would drift into a discussion of some obscure philosophical problem and insist that she try to discuss it too, and she would forget about Jeremy and what he had done.

Lightning flashed overhead. There was a crash of thunder two seconds later. She was soaked to the skin, but she almost welcomed the violence of the weather. For a few seconds at a time it knocked out of her head the catastrophe that was her life. Wouldn't she ever learn? Because the worst of it was that it wasn't just Jeremy. She'd neglected her work at university because she'd spent so much time being business manager of various student drama productions starring Malcolm, her boyfriend. It hadn't been an ideal relationship, but she'd tried hard to make it work; then Malcolm had met the sister of a famous producer and walked out.

Tasha had scraped through her finals somehow and found a job in the teeth of deservedly unenthusiastic references. She'd started at the bottom in the marketing department of a publishing house, working insanely hard to forget about Malcolm, and had soon had a promotion. Just when things had been beginning to look good she'd started going out with Colin, a struggling writer. Colin had moved in with her and forgotten to pay the rent for two years, and then he had married a well-known literary agent. Tasha did not really subscribe to the theory that men were scum, but why did she always end up with the kind of man who thought every relationship involved a certain amount of take and take? She'd found a new job in the marketing and promotions department of a well-known women's magazine, had a *short* disastrous relationship for a change, and then she'd met Jeremy. And now she was twenty-six. Was it going to be like this for the rest of her life?

Blasts of rain battered her face. Tasha scowled. It was stupid dwelling on the past. Stupid to be miserable about things she could do nothing about. The only problem was that it was better than the alternative: being miserable about all the things she was somehow going to *have* to do something about. Finding a new job, for instance, because she'd given notice and her replacement was arriving this week. Finding a place to live at a week's notice, to take another example, because the new tenant of her old flat was due to move in next week and Tasha certainly wasn't going to be living with Jeremy. And last but not least, horror of horrors—*no*. She was *not* going to think about that. She was turning the last bend in the road. Another five minutes, and she would be there.

The house was blazing with lights. If her father couldn't hear the phone, though, chances were he wouldn't hear a knock or doorbell either, and Tasha was too wet and cold to wait to find out. Like all the professor's children, stepchildren, nieces, nephews and third cousins twice removed Tasha had a key. She turned it in the front door, and stepped inside.

She glanced, ruefully, in the hall mirror—she actually looked as bad as she felt, which was saying something.

She would never be conventionally beautiful—her large, misty grey-green eyes were her best feature, but they were set in a face which combined high, broad cheekbones with a pointed chin. Her eyes slanted up slightly under flyaway brows, and on a good day they gave her oddly shaped face a haunting, almost elfin look. On a good day there was something almost other-worldly about her colouring, hair like silver gilt cut along the jaw as a brilliant frame for the misty eyes and pale skin.

Today, however, was emphatically not a good day. Her wet hair clung to her head like dirty, sodden straw; her skin was deathly pale, her small chin just made her face look pinched. Her eyes weren't red from crying because she hadn't been able to cry; they just stared blankly out from the pale, pinched face. It was stupid to care about how she looked at a time like this, except that seeing herself in the mirror, plain, wet, miserable, she could hardly blame

Jeremy for walking away from someone a little rain could turn into a drowned rat.

She grimaced, and headed automatically for the stairs to the top of the house, where her father was no doubt wrestling with a recalcitrant footnote.

There are fathers who deal with a crisis in a daughter's love life by offering to beat her boyfriend to a pulp, or to send her on a package holiday to Hawaii. Then there are fathers who talk thoughtfully about the seventeenth-century philosopher Spinoza, who analysed the emotions according to the rules of geometry. The professor belonged to this smaller category of father, with the result that the emotions he talked about always seemed to exist somewhere off on Planet Philosophy, and to have nothing whatsoever to do with anything anyone might feel in the real world. Tasha's mother had always found this attitude intensely irritating, but Tasha liked it: it made her feel as though nothing in the real world mattered that much. The more unspeakably horrible things were, the more desperately it mattered to be told that they weren't really all that important. Another minute and—well, nothing would be any different, but her father would put an arm around her and say something about his hero and maybe she would feel a little bit better.

She'd already put her foot on the first step when she heard the unmistakable sound of a glass being set on a table.

'Daddy!' she exclaimed, and rushed into the sitting room. 'Daddy, it's me—'

A man was standing by the fireplace with his back to the door.

'I'm afraid he's not here,' he said. 'I got here this morning and there was no sign of him.'

Tasha stared speechlessly as the man turned to face her and give her a familiar sardonic smile. She'd come four miles by bike, two hundred and twenty miles by train and two miles on foot in the pouring rain to be all alone with Bad Cousin Chaz.

Chase Adam Zachary Taggart looked as though he'd stepped out of the kind of ad where tall, loose-limbed, impossibly handsome men run through the streets of Paris at dawn with a good-looking double bass. He was standing with his weight on one leg, hands in his pockets, with loose-limbed easy grace; he was wearing a suit which managed, for all its ravishing dark elegance, to look like a careless afterthought, something to throw on if you had to open a West End show or pick up an Oscar or improvise jazz in a backroom bar—he'd done all three. Black hair swept back from a sardonic face; black eyes looked cynically out at the world from under hooked black brows; a finely carved yet sensuous mouth curved in a faint, cynical smile. He was instinctively graceful, terrifyingly elegant, impossibly handsome and, unlike her bedraggled self, dry.

He was also, Tasha thought resentfully, supposed to be several thousand miles away. She'd done the decent thing and sent him an invitation six months ago to the wedding. Bad Cousin Chaz had replied that, much as he'd love to come, business commitments would make it impossible to get away from New York at that particular time. Company A was going to be taking over Company B, or Company C was launching a flotation of shares, or maybe Chaz had just scheduled the assassination of the director of Company D for the day of the wedding—Tasha couldn't remember precisely which flimsy excuse had formed the substance of the calculated rudeness of the reply. She'd been too relieved. The wedding was to be her special day; it had been wonderful to know for sure that, on that day of all days, Bad Cousin Chaz would not be there.

Except that he was here, now, of all impossible times—

'What are you doing here?' she managed to say at last. 'I thought you were in New York.'

'I was.'

'I thought you couldn't *leave* New York,' Tasha said pointedly. 'I thought the reason you couldn't come to the wedding was that you were going to be expectedly detained on urgent business that couldn't spare you for two hours let alone two days.'

Chaz shrugged. 'Deal's off. Something I wanted to discuss with the professor. I'll have to get back soon, though; 'fraid I can't stay for the wedding.'

He raised a sardonic black eyebrow in a gesture she knew and loathed. 'Speaking of which, what are *you* doing here? You should be ticking off items on "101 Things Every Bride Should Do For a Perfect Wedding", not gallivanting around the countryside.'

Tasha gritted her teeth. He was going to have to know sooner or later; no point fighting off the inevitable.

'Deal's off,' she said curtly.

Chaz had never made any secret of despising Jeremy; she braced herself for some acerbic remark.

He was frowning. 'Off? You mean as in bridesmaids dismissed, cancel the cake?'

'That's right,' said Tasha.

Chaz whistled softly, then grinned. 'Well, let me be the first to congratulate you, Tash, I couldn't be more pleased. What exactly made you change your mind?'

Tasha gritted her teeth again.

'I didn't,' she said.

An astonished swoop of eyebrow met this new development. 'You mean it was *Jeremy's* idea?'

'Yes.'

'Well, don't stop there,' said her abominable cousin. 'Tell me all about it, or, no, wait, let me get you a drink and then tell me all about it. What are you having?'

'Scotch,' said Tasha. 'And it's none of your business.'

Chaz crossed the room to the drinks cupboard. 'Just as you like,' he said, filling two glasses. 'Depends whether you want me to hear your version or someone else's.' He put the drink in her hand, then gestured towards the sofa. 'Come and get dry.'

Tasha sank wearily to the sofa. Chaz sat down beside her, one leg crossed over the other, an arm along the back of the sofa.

'Well, you may as well know,' she said dully. 'You know how Daddy has all those investments?'

'Yes?'

'But he's not one of those rich men people have heard of, and I didn't realise Jeremy knew.'

'Yes?'

'But he did, only he didn't realise—what I mean is, I told him Daddy had decided to give each of us now the money he would have left to us in his will, but I never said he was going to give most of it to that educational trust because it didn't seem relevant. I didn't know Jeremy knew how much Daddy had so I didn't know how much he thought I'd be getting.'

'So he'd done his homework and thought he'd be on first name terms with five or six million pounds instead of a couple of hundred grand?'

'And he said he needed the money to do what he wanted to do, it wasn't for him it was for us, if he couldn't do the things he'd dreamed of accomplishing he wouldn't be the man I thought I was marrying and we'd both be diminished—'

She turned her head away. She wasn't going to cry in front of Chaz.

When her voice was steady again she said, 'It's stupid. I feel ashamed even though I didn't do anything wrong. I feel sick inside. It's as if I've lost someone who never even existed, and I keep seeing his face and hearing his voice saying those things and they won't go away and nothing makes it any better. I don't know what would make it better.'

As long as her head was turned away she could say the things she would have said to her father. Her father would have said something philosophical.

Chaz said, 'Well, I know what I'd do, but it probably isn't your style.'

'What's that?' said Tasha drearily. 'Puncture his tyres?'

'I was thinking more in terms of violent physical exercise,' said Chaz.

'I've already ridden four miles by bicycle and walked two miles in the rain,' said Tasha.

'That wasn't quite the kind of exercise I had in mind,' said Chaz.

Something in his tone of voice made Tasha lift her head. There was a lurking spark of mischief in her cousin's eyes.

'Oh, you mean sleep with someone,' she said baldly. 'I should have known—when do you ever think of anything else?'

'Once in a while,' said Chaz. 'I did say I thought it wasn't your style.'

'It's just that it's such a stupid idea,' said Tasha. 'What am I supposed to do? Walk into a pub or a wine bar or something and proposition the first man I see? Why on *earth* would that make me feel better?'

'I wasn't suggesting you should sleep with just anyone,' said Chaz.

'Well, what *did* you have in mind?' said Tasha in exasperation.

A black eyebrow swooped up mockingly. 'You could spend the night with me.'

Tasha stared at him for a moment—then, to her astonishment, burst out laughing. 'Chaz, you're impossible. Of all the times to be making stupid jokes—'

'It wasn't a joke,' said Chaz. 'It's a serious suggestion in that it would probably make you feel better. Of course it's true I wouldn't expect you to try it, but that doesn't make it a joke.'

Tasha stared at her mad, bad cousin. Except, of course, that he wasn't her cousin. Chase Taggart was the son of the first wife of the second husband, or was it the second wife of the first husband—? No. Tasha's parents had got divorced when she was ten. Her mother, leaving her first husband, had gone to stay briefly with her sister, then on her third. Tasha's Aunt Monica had had a glamorous new husband; the husband had had a son. That son, who was absolutely no relation of Tasha's of any kind, was Chaz: five years older and five thousand years more sophisticated, black-haired, black-eyed, black-browed, with a razor-sharp wit used unsparingly on whichever of his four or five families he happened to visit.

Her mad, bad not-really-cousin stared back at her, eyes brilliant with amusement. 'Well?'

'Well what?' said Tasha.

'Well, what's the answer?'

'The answer is I think you're completely despicable,' snapped Tasha. 'I suppose this is something that's worked for you in the past? You find some woman whose world has fallen apart and who's completely devastated and instead of showing even an iota of sympathy you take advantage of her vulnerable state to seduce her.'

A smile tugged at the corner of his mouth. 'There are different ways of showing sympathy,' said Chaz unrepentantly. 'Anyway, there's a limit to how much sympathy I can feel for you when you've just escaped being sentenced to life with a complete and utter prat. Look on the bright side, at least you'll never have to sleep with Jeremy again, *or* for that matter with that other idiot—what was his name? Oh, yes, Martin, *or* with the one before that—Malcolm, was it? No, I'm getting mixed up, aren't I? Malcolm was your first, then there was Colin, *then* the man like a piece of damp felt—where in God's name do you find them all, Tash? If you've got to fall for a complete loser, why can't you at least pick one who's good in bed?'

Tasha had had plenty of arguments with Chaz over the years, but she hadn't realised how angry it was possible to be. She felt as if the blood in her veins was foaming with fury. 'I'm certainly not going to discuss them with you,' she said coldly. 'I'd just like to point out, though, that you can't possibly know what any of them were like in bed—'

'Sure I can,' Chaz said cheerfully. 'If you think it's self-ish to seduce someone, as you put it, it must be because you think the man is the only one who can enjoy it, which means, sweet coz, that they can't have been doing it right.'

Tasha realised that she was actually grinding her teeth. 'I don't want to discuss it,' she said again, in a tone that had moved from the refrigerator to the freezer.

'Poor darling, was it that bad?' said Chaz, with the same lurking smile. 'Mind you, I had my suspicions—'

'I *don't want to discuss it*,' Tasha said furiously.

'Of course you don't,' said Chaz. 'You'd like to hit me for being right. Completely unfair, if you ask me. After all, I'm not the one who left you bored and frustrated through lack of imagination and sheer technical incompetence—'

Tasha didn't even think. Rage snapped her hand back and sent it slicing through the air at the handsome, taunting face.

A hand shot up and caught her wrist.

'I know you'd like to hit me, Natasha,' Chaz said softly, his deep, slow voice dragging over her name like a caress. 'But don't be too hasty.' His eyes gleamed. 'Here's the deal. Let me kiss you, and if you don't like it you can hit me and I won't hit you back.'

Tasha tried to pull her hand away, but his grip tightened on her wrist.

'Come on, Tash,' he said, the smile lighting his eyes. 'Don't tell me you've never wondered. And it's just a kiss, after all. What are you afraid of? That you might like it too much?'

Tasha glared at him speechlessly.

He laughed. 'Well, let's try unilateral disarmament.' He released her wrist, allowing his hand to fall to his side. 'Come on, Tash,' he said even more softly, an eyebrow quirking up. 'Close your eyes.'

Later she would never know why she did it. Instead of slapping him across the face the moment her hand was free, she let her hand drop harmlessly to her lap and closed her eyes.

At first she thought he'd been teasing her, that it was just a joke to see if she'd do it. Then something brushed her mouth as lightly as the wing of a butterfly, and was gone. It brushed her mouth again; it was as if someone had held a lighted match just short of her mouth, grazing her lips with the scorched air just outside the flame. Then it was gone, but her mouth stung from the fleeting contact. Then it was back, but this time it lingered just the fraction of a second longer before dropping away.

Tasha found that she was holding her breath. The featherlight touch seemed to have nothing to do with her horrible cousin Chaz, who was always so knowing, so arrogant, so convinced that he was a super-stud. Something touched her mouth again, long enough for her to feel the warmth of his breath before it was gone. Her lips parted involuntarily, and now his mouth was on hers and she could taste him, something as smooth and golden as her Scotch, with wickedness lurking in its amber depths. It warmed her like the Scotch, melting a little of the cold, hard core of misery that was like an icy rock in her chest; she breathed in, opening her mouth wider.

The tip of his tongue traced the sensitive skin of her upper lip, leaving it tingling as if from an electric shock—and the inside of the lip tingled too, as if in anticipation. But the tongue was gone, leaving only the memory of the thrill, a longing to feel it again. Now he ran the tip of his tongue just inside her lips, and the reality was better than imagination, intoxicating in its intensity, as if someone had doubled the strength of her drink behind her back. Tasha breathed out on a long sigh, relaxing into the kiss; the lovely honeyed warmth spread through her body, dissolving the wretchedness—or maybe just shielding her for the moment from its bitter cold. But even if it was just for the moment what did it matter? She let her mouth melt against his, savouring the heady taste of it.

He drew his mouth away, and she waited to feel his mouth on hers again, but this time it did not come back.

'You can open your eyes now, Tasha,' Chaz said softly.

She opened her eyes. It was a shock to see Chaz looking just as he always did; she might have thought she'd imagined those butterfly kisses, but his mouth was still moist. It was smiling slightly; if she put her mouth on his she would feel the smile on her lips.

She felt slightly sick. The warmth, the lovely sense that nothing mattered except the here and now, had gone with the kiss; the hard, cold rock was back inside.

She stared at Chaz as if she were seeing him for the first time, taking in the humorous, supple mouth, the brilliant black eyes under the black slash of brow, the hawk-like nose and hard jaw.

'So how was it for you, darling?' he asked, one of the eyebrows quirking up.

'It was—' Tasha began. She was still staring at him.

'You were right,' she said. 'I was completely wrong. It has nothing to do with feelings; it's just a question of technique. You must have practised a lot to be so good.'

Chaz started to say something and then stopped. He said slowly, 'So you don't want to hit me, Tash?'

Tasha was still staring at him. 'No,' she said. 'I want to sleep with you.'

Chaz stared at her. 'You what?'

'It was your idea,' Tasha reminded him. 'And you're right. It's just a physical thing, after all. We can enjoy it for what it is and forget about it. It will help me to forget about all this.'

An odd, rueful expression crept onto the supremely self-confident face of the man beside her. 'Oh, Lord,' he said.

'Daddy won't be back for ages. I'm still on the pill. We can just go upstairs now,' said Tasha. 'Or would you rather have another drink first?'

Chaz took her hand in his, running his thumb over her palm. The honeyed warmth pooled in the palm of her hand and spread up her arm; she drew in a sharp breath.

'Tash, darling,' said Chaz, 'I know it was my idea, but it probably wasn't a very good one.'

'Why not?' said Tasha. 'Don't you think you'd enjoy it?'

'Yes, but—'

'Don't you think I'd enjoy it?'

'Yes, but—'

'Then what's the problem?' Tasha said impatiently.

He smiled at her wryly. 'I think you'd hate yourself and me afterwards. You probably can't hate me any more than you do already, but—'

'I don't hate you, Chaz,' Tasha interrupted ruthlessly, conveniently ignoring her conviction for the past sixteen years that Chaz was a blot on the planet. 'I just think you're selfish and afraid of commitment. Are you afraid I'll come chasing you afterwards?'

'No, I'm not afraid of that.' His thumb was still stroking her palm. 'I just think you're taking on more than you can deal with at a time when you're pretty vulnerable.' He raised an eyebrow in self-mockery. 'I'll probably hate myself for this, but I don't think I should take advantage of what's obviously a momentary aberration.'

Tasha stared at him blankly. If he was going to talk about momentary aberrations, when had Chaz ever turned down anyone who was willing? It must be because she was so unattractive.

'I know I look horrible,' she said, 'but it's just because I got wet. I'll look a lot better when I've dried off.'

'You look bloody marvellous,' said Chaz, 'but the answer is no.'

'Is it because you think I'm no good in bed?' asked Tasha.

Chaz gave her another rueful smile. 'Tash, darling,' he said, 'I don't think that, and I'd love to have the chance to find out, but in case you hadn't noticed I'm being chivalrous for the first time in my life.'

Tasha lay wearily back against the sofa. Just for a minute she'd thought she could escape the leaden weight in her chest. For an hour, maybe a couple of hours, that lovely golden warmth would have spread through her body and maybe for just a little while she could have put everything out of her mind as well. But she was just stuck with it. A tear trickled down her cheek.

Chaz wiped it away with a finger. 'I may be good, but I'm not *that* good,' he said.

'I'd love to have the chance to find out,' Tasha said pointedly. 'I don't call it very chivalrous to lead me on and then back out at the last minute. I'll bet you'd be furious if a woman did that to you and then told you it was for your own good.'

'*Touché,*' said Chaz, 'but I still think you'd regret it.' He smiled at her. 'Tell you what. Pretend I'm really your cousin, pretend you don't think to know me is to loathe me, and I'll give you a shoulder to cry on.'

He slid one arm behind her shoulders, the other under her knees, and scooped her up onto his lap. His strong arms closed tight around her; her legs lay across his powerful thighs, she could hear his heart beating in the powerful chest. 'Is that better?' he asked, his breath stirring her hair.

It was and it wasn't. The sheer physical strength and solidity of the body which held hers was a comfort, keeping at bay a little of the misery. But it made her whole body ache with a yearning which couldn't be satisfied.

'It's a bit better,' said Tasha.

'Good,' said Chaz.

'But could you not hold me quite so tight?'

'Sorry,' said Chaz. He loosened his arms.

'Thanks,' said Tasha. She put her arms around his neck. Chaz looked at her warily.

Tasha looked at the firm, sensuous mouth. 'Do you think I'll regret it if I kiss you?' she asked.

An eyebrow quirked up. 'No,' he said wryly. 'But I may.'

Tasha smiled. 'You can look after yourself,' she said, and she kissed him full on the mouth.

There was a fraction of a second in which he hesitated, probably wondering whether it was chivalrous to take advantage of her vulnerable state of mind.

Tasha had already worked out that she'd better make the most of her chances, now that it turned out Chaz had this previously unsuspected streak of chivalry in his character. She couldn't waste time on little butterfly kisses when any minute chivalry might raise its ugly head; she devoured his

mouth the way a man downs his last drink before closing
time.

Chivalry went to the wall.

His arms tightened around her again; his mouth opened
under hers, and he responded to the urgency of her kisses
with a hungry passion which showed, she realised dimly,
how much restraint he must have been showing earlier. She
buried her hands in his hair, holding his head so he couldn't
move it, and raised her head so that she could look into the
face of her mad, bad kissing cousin. Now her eyes devoured his face as hungrily as her mouth had devoured his
mouth. When she'd kissed her boyfriends physical imper-
fections hadn't seemed to matter, because she'd always
thought she was kissing someone with a wonderful character. Chaz, on the other hand, was selfish and bad tem-
pered and had countless bad qualities without a single one
to redeem them—but he was so beautiful. She kissed one
corner of his mouth, then the other, tucking her tongue into
the crease. He smiled, so that the corner of his mouth
quirked up under hers, and then he kissed the corner of her
mouth, still smiling, and slid his tongue into her mouth.

Instead of the honeyed warmth she felt something hotter
and sweeter, as fiery as a slug of brandy. Her misery did
not melt this time from her mind—it was blasted out of it.
There was nothing but the taste of his mouth, the hard
muscle of his body—that, and the feeling that lava ran in
her veins. She lost all sense of time. All that mattered was
the scorching heat that flared up at his touch, burning away
all thought—and the intoxicating awareness that she had
the same effect on him. Chaz was always so mocking, so
cool, so superior—but now his heart pounded next to hers,
and she could hear his breath coming in ragged gasps. His
hand dropped to her thigh, forcing her up against his hips
so that she could feel his desire for her.

At last he raised his hands to her shoulders and held her away.

'You're right,' he said. 'This is insane. Let's go upstairs.'

Tasha looked into his face. His hair had fallen forward over one eyebrow; his eyes were brilliant, his mouth slightly smiling. She hadn't known it was possible to want a man so badly. But there were other passions boiling up inside her too. She had somehow been polite and civilised to Jeremy, she'd had to walk away from what she'd thought was a whole lifetime with the perfect man, someone who'd turned out not to exist. There was rage just below the surface for men who pretended they wanted something for your good, men who changed the rules as soon as they saw something they wanted. Sitting across Chaz's lap, she could feel the tension in his body, feel the desire just barely held in check.

'I don't think that's a very good idea,' said Tasha, jumping to her feet.

*'What?'* said Chaz.

'I think you'd hate yourself afterwards,' Tasha explained cheerfully. Her pulse was still racing at about twice its normal speed; the look on his face at this riposte did nothing to slow it down.

'Very funny,' said Chaz.

'I think you were right,' Tasha said. 'I'm in a very vulnerable state of mind. You'd regret it if you felt you'd taken advantage of me.'

Temper sizzled in the black eyes. The lovely, sensuous mouth tightened ominously.

'All right,' said Chaz. 'You've made your point. Satisfied?' He stood up, thrust his hands in his pockets, and made an effort to shrug off his irritation. 'I admit it was patronising,' he said. 'But we both want the same thing, after all.' He smiled at her, running a finger over her kiss-swollen mouth. 'Fireworks,' he said softly. 'Let's go up-stairs and set some off.'

Tasha looked up at him. He was right in a way. All these years she'd despised him for being unfair to her boyfriends, for judging them by superficial standards—she was just be-ginning to realise that she hadn't even understood what he was talking about. She could go upstairs and find out with a vengeance.

But there were still other passions raging inside her. It was wonderful to have Chaz standing there, furious at her but not able to stay furious because he wanted her so badly. When would she ever have a chance like this again? Whereas if she wanted to sleep with him, she thought flip-pantly, she could do that any time.

Chaz was still smiling. Of course, he could see the way she was looking at him, eyes lingering on the mouth she had kissed; how could he imagine she wouldn't give in?

If she were her usual self of course she would give in. But where had being her usual self got her? She knew she was behaving badly; it felt wonderful to *know* she was be-having badly and do it anyway. She was going to be a bad, bad, bad, bad girl.

'I'd just rather not,' said Tasha, and hugged herself at the look of blank incredulity that replaced the confident smile.

'You're actually serious about this,' Chaz said slowly.

'Of course I'm serious about it,' said Tasha.

A muscle twitched in his cheek. 'I should take you over my knee and spank you for this,' he said tightly. 'And I'm quite serious about that, in case you're wondering.'

'I don't know why,' Tasha shot back. 'You backed out and I didn't threaten you with physical violence; why is this any different?'

'The difference,' Chaz said acidly, 'is that you're doing it out of sheer bloody-mindedness.'

'I know,' Tasha said with disconcerting frankness. 'But it feels so lovely.'

'Is that meant to make me feel better about it?' asked Chaz.

'I'm upset,' said Tasha. 'My life has been turned upside down. It may not be your fault, but you're here. It's not fair, but then life isn't fair.' She gave him a dazzling smile. 'Anyway, who knows when I'll have another chance to be bloody-minded to you? Whereas there's a good chance I can sleep with you some other time if I want to. Unless, of course, you decide you want your revenge.'

'Oh, for God's sake—' He scowled at her.

'You know, we could go on like this for years,' Tasha said blithely. 'Next time you could proposition me and turn me down when I accept, then I could proposition you and then change my mind, then you could start to seduce me and then have a headache—'

'Will you stop it?' There was still a glint of temper in the black eyes, but a reluctant smile tugged at the corner of his mouth. 'I don't know whether to kiss you or kill you,' he said exasperatedly.

'Well, you'd better not kiss me,' said Tasha. 'I wouldn't want you to get excited.'

Chaz gave her a sardonic look. 'You know, the funny thing is people have quite the wrong idea of you. Everyone thinks you're such a nice girl.'

'Yes,' Tasha said rather bitterly. 'That's why they walk all over me.'

'No comment,' said Chaz. 'I'm going to have another drink to calm my nerves.'

He walked over to the sideboard. Tasha followed him. She could do with a drink herself. It occurred to her that she'd never been so horrible to anyone in her whole life. For some reason she liked Chaz a lot better now that she'd been so horrible to him.

'I enjoyed the kiss, anyway,' she said politely. 'Both kisses.'

Chaz flicked her a glance. 'I could tell.' An eyebrow shot up. 'Me too. Let's not pursue that line of thought, shall we?'

He poured out a drink for himself, and one for Tasha.

He lifted his glass. 'To what might have been,' he said.

'To what might have been,' Tasha said gloomily. She took a sip of her drink.

For about the two-hundredth time in twenty-four hours her mind turned to composition. It was struggling with a communication which was sometimes a letter starting 'I am sorry to say', and sometimes a repulsively formal printed invitation retraction starting 'Professor G.G. Merrill regrets to inform you', but which *always* got bogged down at 'that'. 'I am sorry to say', she began, decided again that the printed formal version worked better, decided again that it would be repulsively formal, and abandoned the debate for the two-hundredth time to try to think of a new job to try for. In a week. When she had nowhere to live and nowhere to put her things. Tasha took another sip of her drink.

If she stored them with her father, she thought again, she would have to move them twice, and anyway he had nowhere to put them. If she stored them with her mother she would get a long lecture on scaring men away and anyway her mother had nowhere to put them because her house was full of wedding presents. *Wedding presents!* For the two-hundredth time she remembered that she was going to have to do something about the wedding presents. She took another sip of her drink, scowling.

She was going to have to *say* something about the presents when she wrote to people so they would know they would get them back. But she would have to say that they should not expect to get them back too soon because she had to look for a new job and a place to stay. But you couldn't say that; you just *couldn't*. But she just *couldn't* send them back until she had a job and a place to stay. But what if it took weeks or months and she still hadn't sent back the presents? But what if—?

'It's going to be so *horrible*,' she said. 'I gave notice on my flat and someone else is moving in so I've nowhere to stay. I gave notice at work so I could work in Jeremy's venture capital company and now I don't have a job. On top of which we've invited hundreds of people to the wedding. Now I'll have to uninvite them and send back hundreds of presents and explain and explain and explain... What is it?'

Chaz was staring down at her with an arrested expression. 'I've had an idea,' he said. 'Just when is this wedding?'

'Next week,' said Tasha with a grimace.

'Not a problem,' said Chaz. 'Special licence.'

'You don't need a licence to call off a wedding,' Tasha said wearily.

'I know that,' said Chaz. The black eyes were brilliant with amusement. 'But I don't think you should call it off.'

'I don't have any choice in the matter,' Tasha said impatiently. 'Even if Jeremy changed his mind I just couldn't after what he said—'

Chaz shook his head. 'Oh, you can't marry Jeremy,' he said. 'That would *never* do.' He smiled at her blandly. 'I think you should go ahead with the wedding, and marry me instead.'

# CHAPTER TWO

'WHAT did you say?' said Tasha.

'You should marry me,' said Chaz. 'It's obvious, really. Can't think why I didn't think of it before.'

Tasha could think of about five million reasons not to marry Chaz. 'Are you out of your mind?' she said feebly.

Chaz gave her a faintly malicious smile. 'Not at all,' he said blandly. 'Only trying to help. It solves everything.'

'Don't be ridiculous,' said Tasha. 'I couldn't possibly marry you.'

'Oh, not permanently, of course,' said Chaz. 'Just for a year or two. Everyone will be *expecting* it to break up, so they won't be surprised—the only thing that they'll be surprised about is that we married in the first place.'

'Exactly,' said Tasha. 'Because it's a ridiculous idea.'

Chaz raised an eyebrow. 'You're not thinking,' he said. 'If you call off the wedding you don't have to give the guests the real reason, but you'll have to explain to your father, no?'

'Yes,' said Tasha.

'Are you sure you want to do that?'

Tasha stared at him. Ever since she'd talked to Jeremy the only thing she'd been able to think of was her father—of throwing herself into his arms and crying her heart out and explaining what had gone wrong. Now, for the first time, she thought of her father's reaction to hearing the reason for the break-up. What if he felt guilty for not giving her more money? What if he thought she was *blaming* him for not giving her more money?

Tasha bit her lip.

'Quite,' said Chaz. 'It's a pretty big burden to ask him to bear. This way we can give the same story to everyone. We ran into each other somewhere and fell madly in love; you broke off your engagement with Jeremy and decided to marry me instead. We knew it was short notice but since the wedding had already been planned we decided to go ahead with it.'

He grinned at her. 'The beauty of it is in the arrangements. Knowing you, I'll bet you've ended up inviting all five of my fractional families—which means the groom's guests are already taken care of apart from a few friends. That just leaves Jeremy's side. Well, they're his guests— let *him* uninvite them. If any of them happen to show up we'll simply make them welcome—we can afford to be generous on our big day.'

Tasha was giggling in spite of herself. The thought of various of Jeremy's repulsive relations sitting in their pews and seeing Chaz at her side appealed to the nasty side of her nature which she hadn't known she had.

'That *is* a temptation,' she admitted. 'In fact, it would be quite helpful, because then they could pick up their gifts on the way out.'

Chaz laughed. 'That's the spirit. Then you can come to New York with me, and file for a divorce in a year.'

Tasha sighed. 'I wish it were that simple.'

Chaz flicked up an eyebrow. 'What's complicated? The most important thing is not to upset your father. The second most important thing is to make things easy for yourself. Well, you've done all the work for the wedding, it's easier to go ahead than do all the extra work of calling it off.' He smiled at her. 'I know it may be a bit hard for you to go through it as a charade when you thought it would be for real, but I'll see you through it. It won't be as bad as you think. And afterwards you can just leave everything behind. Spend a year in New York, where there's nothing to remind

you of Jeremy or the things you planned to do. At the end
of the year make up your mind what to do next.'

Tasha ran a hand absent-mindedly through her hair. For
the first time she considered the preposterous suggestion as
a serious possibility. There was no doubt about it; it would
be far simpler to go through with things at this stage than
to pull back. But how could she marry Chaz?

'Even if all that's true,' she said at last, 'why would you
do such a thing? You can't possibly want to be married.
It'll put a terrible cramp in your style.'

Chaz shrugged. 'True enough.' The black eyes were
thoughtful. 'But your father's been pretty decent to me.
He's certainly the nearest thing I've ever had to a father,
and I don't have many chances to do something for him.'
His mouth quirked up. 'Besides, Tash, you've always been
the most amusing of all my ragbag of sort-of relations, and
there's not much I won't do for people who don't bore me.'

Tasha stared at him. 'But you hate me,' she protested.

'You hate me,' Chaz corrected her gently. 'But your passion is unrequited.' He gave her a gleaming glance. 'And,
if I may say so, misplaced. You don't have to put me in
your top ten for this, but I expect you to give me credit,
for once, for doing something not purely out of self-
interest.'

Tasha still had her drink in her hand. She finished the
glass absent-mindedly and set it down.

She frowned. 'I don't know,' she said. 'I've never slept
with anyone I wasn't in love with. I know I said I was
going to a little while ago but I'm not really myself today.
I have a feeling when I'm myself again it will just seem
impossible again. I don't want you to get the wrong idea.'

She glanced up again, forcing herself to meet his eyes.
Chaz gave her a rather wry smile. 'I don't have the wrong
idea,' he said. 'I always said it wasn't your style. It's an
unconditional offer, Tash; you don't have to sleep with me

if you don't want to.' An amused eyebrow shot up as a thought struck him. 'Anyway, if I start committing adultery a couple of weeks after the wedding it'll give you ironclad grounds for divorce, and God knows the temptation will be there—all the women I didn't marry will have their hatchets out for you, darling, and be only too happy to remind me of what I let slip.'

Tasha realised that she was feeling unreasonably annoyed by this remark. It was completely ridiculous. If she went through with it she couldn't expect Chaz to remain celibate for a year to honour a paper marriage, and she had absolutely no right to be jealous of him. The comment was the type of cynical, sophisticated remark that had always irritated her, but the chances were his assessment of the situation was actually right; it was ridiculous to hold it against him for knowing his world. The bottom line was that he was being very generous, offering her a way out of a nightmarish situation without asking anything in return.

Without asking *anything* in return? *Chaz?*

'Well, if you don't want sex what do you want?' asked Tasha.

Chaz grinned. 'I didn't say I didn't want it, darling. I just said you didn't have to oblige.'

'Exactly,' said Tasha. 'So what do you expect from me? Is it enough to know you're protecting Daddy from something you think he shouldn't know? Or do you want something more?'

Chaz paused for thought. 'Well, if we split up I want half the wedding presents,' he said. 'I've always wanted to run a five-toaster flat; I reckon we can count on a good ten even without Jeremy's side.'

'I did have a wedding list,' Tasha pointed out.

'Did you? How disappointing. Well, bags the toaster if we only get one.'

Tasha smiled in spite of herself. 'Will you be serious?'

she asked. 'I just want to know what I'm getting into. If there's something you want out of this I'd rather know now.'

Chaz shrugged. 'No strings attached, if that's what you mean. When I say unconditional I mean unconditional. You could keep me company at a few boring dinners, but if you can't face it I shan't mind. You don't have to pretend to be in love with me when we're out together in public. Half the women I know married for money; no one will think the worse of you if they think you did—they'll just think you did well for yourself to get someone who wasn't physically repulsive into the bargain.'

Tasha grimaced. 'But that's horrible,' she said. 'How can you stand it?'

'Stand what?'

'Living with all those miserable people,' said Tasha.

Chaz raised a sardonic eyebrow. 'Who says they're miserable? They sell the one thing they have for the one thing they want—it's not a bad deal.'

Tasha shuddered. What was the use of all that money, she thought, if someone had a whole life without love? But she certainly wasn't going to argue about that with Chaz.

'So what's the verdict?' said Chaz. 'Do you want to give it a whirl?'

Tasha looked at him doubtfully. It wouldn't be a real marriage, of course, but what on earth would it be like to live for a whole year with Chaz? He could be charming when he chose, but there was a cynical side to his character that always made her want to hit him. What would it be like to live with someone who always thought the worst of everyone? On the other hand if she didn't, what could she tell her father?

'Well,' she said.

Chaz sipped his drink, looking up at her from under Satanic eyebrows, the sardonic expression more pronounced. She had the impression he knew exactly what she was thinking.

She had to do something. Tasha closed her eyes, and she saw a list of hundreds of wedding guests, and three rooms full of wedding presents. If she said no she would have to write to all those guests in the next two days. Some had already made expensive and non-refundable travel arrangements...

She opened her eyes. Chaz was still watching her. He really was devastatingly handsome, she thought irrelevantly. It was hard to believe she'd actually kissed him about ten minutes ago.

'All right,' said Tasha. 'I accept.'

'Against your better judgement,' Chaz said acutely. 'Poor darling. Marriage to the Archfiend versus one thousand disappointed guests.' He smiled at her, the slightly crooked, uncynical smile that was so disarming because so seldom seen. 'Never mind, Tash, I'll try to see you don't regret it.'

'I'm sure I shan't regret it,' Tasha said stoutly if untruthfully.

'Liar,' said her husband-to-be. His eyes were bright with amusement. 'Don't look so despondent, darling. We're in this together. We'll have a marvellous time. First but not least the wedding—I've managed to avoid playing the lead in one for thirty-one years, but if I've got to start I can't imagine a better way than as an understudy. Then there's my family, most of whom I haven't seen in donkey's years—you can't avoid all of the people all of the time, but you can avoid most of the people most of the time, and since you are deservedly and unreservedly adored by all I'll enjoy a brief return to favour as the prodigal—followed by a complete severance of relations, with any luck, when I'm unfaithful to their darling within a month of the wedding...'

Tasha suppressed a smile. It was certainly true that the family were going to see marriage as an unexpected sign of good behaviour on the part of their most disgraceful member. 'You're so cynical,' she said. 'People have been saying to me for years that you weren't bad at heart, you just hadn't found what you were looking for, that if you just found the right woman it would make all the difference. They'll just be happy because they'll think you've found the right person. It's not their fault that it's not true.'

The black eyes gleamed. 'It sounds just the sort of thing they would say,' he said sardonically. 'No surprises there. The question is, Tash darling, what did you say back?'

He gave a shout of laughter at her embarrassed expression. 'Unrepeatable, was it?' he said, grinning. 'Thought so. Let's see, I'll bet you said if I ever did find the right woman heaven help the woman.'

'I don't remember what I said,' said Tasha.

'How convenient,' said Chaz, with a gleaming glance. 'Well, it's what I'd say, so I don't see why you shouldn't. But enough of me. We have something to celebrate.'

'*Do* we?' said Tasha.

'Sure we do,' said Chaz. 'This calls for champagne. Does your father have champagne?'

'No,' said Tasha.

'Well, let's stick to Scotch, then,' said Chaz. 'We seem to have done all right on it so far.'

He filled their glasses.

He raised his own. 'To Jeremy,' he said. 'The word ''cad'' has gone out of fashion, but the behaviour never goes out of style. Here's hoping he gets what's coming to him.'

'That's a horrible toast,' said Tasha.

'But one from the heart,' said Chaz, looking uncharacteristically grim.

'Well, I'm not going to drink to it,' said Tasha.

Chaz smiled at her. 'Well, propose your own, then.'

'All right, I will,' said Tasha. She gave him a mischievous smile, and raised her glass. 'To the right woman, heaven help her.'

Chaz laughed. 'Well, I'll drink to that.' A sardonic eyebrow flicked up. 'To the right woman, heaven help her,' he repeated, raising his glass, and he drained it at a single swallow.

# CHAPTER THREE

IN THE days that followed Tasha was to find herself looking back on that evening with blank incredulity. She'd been upset, yes. She'd had a couple of stiff drinks, yes. That still didn't explain how she'd come to kiss Chaz and enjoy it, let alone agree to the most insane proposition she'd ever heard of in her life. The most likely explanation was that she had, in fact, been temporarily insane. The problem was, once she'd agreed to the suggestion in a moment of derangement she was stuck with it when sanity returned.

Chaz had not only had to pay a lot of money for the special licence. He had also had to find a bishop and persuade him that the circumstances requiring the licence were seriously special—on a par with, say, the groom being called off to fight for his country at short notice. Given that he had been able to talk Tasha into it in the first place it was perhaps not surprising that he was able to talk a bishop around as well, but Tasha had a feeling it had not been as easy as he had made it sound.

He had then commandeered the guest list and taken it upon himself to notify all guests of the change. To cancel the wedding now would involve not only notifying everyone again, but explaining how she had come to acquire and discard a new fiancé in a few days' time. She just didn't feel up to it.

She found the actual wedding much harder to bear than she had expected.

When Chaz had made the suggestion she'd thought only of the invitations she wouldn't have to retract, the problem of having to live with Chaz for a year afterwards. It wasn't until she was actually walking down the aisle on her father's arm that she remembered the comment Chaz had made, that she'd go through as a charade something she'd expected to be for real.

The whole point of marrying Chaz, after all, had been to avoid upsetting the arrangements. The result, naturally, was that the wedding was in every detail exactly what it would have been if she had been marrying the man she'd expected, only last week, to be spending the rest of her life with.

The dress was obviously the same. It had a bodice of white beadwork that glinted in the soft filmy fabric like tiny pearls, and a long narrow skirt of layers and layers of the same filmy white. Putting it on, she had not been able to help remembering the day she had chosen it, the endless fittings she'd undergone, imagining always the day when Jeremy would see this vision of loveliness walk down the aisle towards him. Now the vision of loveliness was walking up to Chaz, who she suspected would take a completely cynical view anyway.

The jonquils and paper-white narcissus on the pews were just what she'd wanted for a spring wedding, and lining the benches were all the innocent guests she'd invited, for whose benefit she was staging the performance. Quite a lot of the people there had been married to each other at one time or another. She could see why Chaz was so cynical about the whole thing, but she'd taken it seriously. She had practised saying the words she would say, words she wouldn't have said if she hadn't meant them. Except that now she was going to say them anyway...

Her bridesmaids paced behind her in the dresses they'd chosen, laughing over colour schemes and designs. The flower girls paced behind them in the tiny dresses she'd chosen for them. She'd never realised how many decisions had to be made in organising a wedding; she'd spent months trying to get everything just right, and all for an empty show.

She had reached the head of the aisle. Chaz was standing there waiting. His eyes met hers, a spark of mischief in them. Well, men didn't fantasise about their weddings; even as a little girl she'd been imagining hers, and she'd never thought she would stand here with someone she didn't love. All the same, that conspiratorial glance had warmed her; here was the one person for whom she didn't have to pretend. Here was someone who knew what she was going through—who'd known better than she had herself what this would be like.

The minister was asking whether anyone could show any just cause why these two should not be joined together. Tasha would have liked to stop the whole thing then and there, but she stayed standing in front of him.

'I require and charge you both, as ye will answer at the dreadful day of judgement when the secrets of all hearts shall be disclosed, that if either of you know any impediment, why ye may not be lawfully joined together in Matrimony, ye do now confess it.'

Tasha gritted her teeth. Why, oh, why had she said she would do this?

The minister read inexorably on. Chaz said 'I will' with an air of patient politeness. Tasha repeated the words mechanically. And now they had come to point of no return.

'I Chase Adam Zachary Taggart take thee Natasha Susan Merrill to my wedded wife....'

Chaz progressed through a long series of vows he'd gone out of his way to avoid heretofore, and certainly had no intention of keeping, with aplomb.

Then it was Tasha's turn. 'I Natasha Susan Merrill,' she whispered, 'take thee Chase Adam Zachary Taggart to my wedded husband...'

Somehow she managed to pronounce the words.

'I pronounce that they be Man and Wife together,' said the minister. 'You may kiss the bride.'

Chaz brushed her mouth with his lips.

'Well done,' he said softly. 'Not too much longer now.'

Soon they were walking back down the aisle. It was done now. Maybe one day she would meet a man she loved and marry him, but if they had a ceremony she would know that she'd been through it before, and lied.

Then there was about an hour outside the church with the photographer. After the sham ceremony the perfectionism of the photographer was almost unbearable; first this group, then that, then about twenty different positions of her and Chaz, just as if anyone would ever care enough about this wedding to open a photo album and look at the pictures. He was just doing his job, of course. He had no way of knowing that there would never be children to leaf through an album, laughing at the old-fashioned nineties clothes, looking at their parents when they were young and in love... There would never be grandchildren looking through the yellowed pages, trying to imagine their parents' grey-haired parents when they were a young and handsome couple...

Chaz glanced down at the woebegone face beneath the veil. They were standing to one side while the photographer took shots of the parents of the happy couple. This was taking some time, since two out of the four had not been on speaking terms for years and arrangement of the party was a delicate business.

'You all right?' Chaz asked.

Tasha nodded.

'Well, if you say so.' A sardonic eyebrow flicked up. 'Fifty pounds says you're thinking of all the adorable children who'd be looking at this rubbish if it were the real thing.'

'It wouldn't be rubbish if it were the real thing,' Tasha hissed.

'Tash, darling,' said Chaz, sounding impossibly bored. 'If it were the real thing you'd have a lot of pictures of you with a man passionately in love with six million pounds you don't happen to have. The only good thing you could hope for in those circumstances would be that there wouldn't be any children left sitting in the wreckage afterwards. You can't make it the real thing by feeling the right thing at the right time, so stop wallowing in sentimentality.'

Tasha glared at him. 'I'm not.'

'No?'

Before she could crush him with a retort, they were swept off to the reception. Hundreds and hundreds of guests shook their hands. A substantial proportion whispered in Tasha's ear how glad they were to see Chaz had found the right woman at last.

Then it was time to wander around the reception greeting people. Chaz stayed close by her side, murmuring wicked comments about people just out of earshot and providing a running commentary on the proceedings. At one point an elderly gentleman came up and shook Chaz's hand.

'Well, you won't remember me,' he said bluffly. 'It's Mr Phipps.'

'Mr Phipps,' Chaz said suavely. 'Of course.'

'Oh, you won't remember,' said Mr Phipps. 'But it's good to see you. Good of you to invite me. To tell you the truth I wouldn't have recognised you, Jeremy—but then that's often the way, as I always tell my boys. Sometimes the plainest little devils you could imagine turn into real ladykillers, heh, heh, heh.'

'Is that a fact?' said Chaz, with a perfectly straight face.

'Well, life is full of surprises,' said Mr Phipps. 'But I won't keep you.' He wandered off in search of the buffet.

'I wonder if it's true,' said Tasha. 'After all, you were beautiful from the day you were born.'

'You weren't born when I was born,' said Chaz.

'I've seen pictures,' said Tasha. 'For all we know, all the ladykillers he thinks plain boys have grown into have been impostors.'

'For all you know someone could have faked those pictures,' he pointed out. 'It isn't true of you, anyway.'

'I know,' Tasha said with a grimace. 'I was nothing much to look at then, and I never grew out of it.'

An eyebrow swooped up in exaggerated scepticism. 'Fishing for compliments, Tash? You were lovely then; you must know you're lovely now. I'm happy to say it if you'd like to hear it.'

Tasha stared at him in astonishment.

'Natasha the fairy princess,' he said mockingly. 'Corny but true. Look at your hair. What colour is it? It's not blonde, or brown, or red. It's got threads of gold and silver and copper that catch the light, and every time the light changes your hair changes with it... And look at your eyes. What colour are they? You might as well ask what colour is water. Green? Silver? Depends on the light.'

He looked at her with narrowed eyes, as if trying to bring her into focus. 'The funny thing is, it never comes out in photographs at all. I've never seen a picture of you that wasn't terrible. It's as if there really was something magical about it, something the camera can't catch.'

Tasha was struck literally speechless. She couldn't believe Chaz could actually mean this seriously—he had to be making fun of her. But he didn't *seem* to be joking. But if she took it seriously he'd probably burst out laughing because she'd swallowed it.

'You don't believe me?' he said. 'I knew there was a jinx on cameras; don't tell me it works on mirrors as well?'

'I—I,' she stammered. 'That is, we—we'd better go in to dinner.'

The seating for the dinner had been one of those problems which make a bride wonder whether there isn't something to be said for elopement. Jeremy's side of the family had been all right; he came with a complement of two parents, both speaking to each other. They might not have had a lot to say, but they didn't snub each other and they didn't insult each other.

On Tasha's side, on the other hand, were her father, her mother, her father's second wife, her father's second wife's third husband—the marriage to Professor Merrill hadn't lasted, but they wouldn't miss Natasha's wedding for *worlds*. There were also her mother's third husband, her mother's second husband and her mother's second husband's third wife—the marriage to her mother hadn't lasted, but they wouldn't miss little Natasha's wedding for *worlds*. There were also Aunt Monica and her five husbands—the third, of course, being Chaz's father as well, though this had not been uppermost in her mind when struggling with the seating plan. There were sundry former and current wives who had always had a soft spot for little Natasha—including, as it happened, Chaz's mother, though again this had not been uppermost in her mind when devising a seating plan. There were lots and lots of more or less connected children.

It wasn't that she *wanted* an ex-rated wedding—but there wasn't a single person there who hadn't made a point of calling her, when his or her own marriage was on the rocks, to say how much they'd always liked her, how much they hoped she wouldn't drop out of sight just because the formal connection wasn't there. There was no one who wouldn't be mortally hurt if left out, or even relegated to a table for friends of the family. Well, what had she been *supposed* to do?

She had finally worked out a plan which placed each person between two other persons of the opposite sex with whom that person was not going to exchange insults. The change of groom had meant that about eight hours of solid anguish had been for nothing. Chaz's parents obviously had to sit next to him, which meant that the whole meticulously calculated plan fell apart and had had to be started from scratch.

In the end she had just put names in a hat and dealt them out. She was *not* going through that again. Sure enough three sworn enemies were now sitting side by side; she sat between Chaz and her father, confidently expecting an explosion.

To her surprise, none came. On the principle that my enemy's enemy is my friend, everyone seemed to have discovered common ground in their previously undisclosed loathing of Jeremy. Up and down the table people could be heard agreeing that better late than never. The closest anyone came to a nasty remark was the heartfelt wish, by Chaz's mother, that *she* had had the sense to trade up before walking down the aisle.

'Still, darling, you wouldn't be here if I *had*, so perhaps it's all for the best,' she concluded cheerfully, blithely ignoring a black look from the man who should have got away.

Tasha almost wished they would all start fighting. She ate her way through the dinner, shrinking further and further into her chair, while the marital veterans called out more or less cynical pieces of advice. 'Don't make the mistake I made,' they would begin, and then explain how it had all gone wrong and how she or Chaz could avoid this. Basically the mistake was to assume it would last for ever: what you were supposed to do was *assume* something was going to go wrong, *assume* a marriage was going to break up unless you watched it every single second to patch it up again as soon as cracks started to show.

If she'd been marrying someone she loved, and who loved her in return, she might have stood up to them, or at least believed something else was possible. But how could she believe that with the kind of marriage she'd ended up with? It was as if the one thing she'd always wanted was the one thing she could never have. She'd spent most of her childhood and adolescence on the sidelines of relationships going wrong, waiting for things to fall apart and then finding herself suddenly in the middle of a brand new family being polite to the complete strangers who were now married to her parents. Her father had tried to provide an element of stability, but she'd wanted more than an *element* of stability. All she'd ever wanted was something she knew was going to last. Maybe they were right, and that was the one thing you could never have and never know.

Chaz glanced down at his drooping bride, then around the table at their relatives. He rapped on his glass with a knife. 'Order, order,' he said. He looked coolly round their startled faces, then laughed suddenly. 'You're giving Tasha the horrors,' he said. 'Stop it, all of you. The next one to mention a prenuptial contract gets sent out of the room.'

There was a little ripple of laughter.

'*Sorry*, darling,' said Tasha's mother. 'You know we just want what's best for you, and you know what they say; an ounce of prevention—'

Chaz silenced her with a look.

'I may have missed something in the ceremony just now,' he said. 'I don't remember anything about covering my back or making sure Tasha didn't take advantage of me. The only things I can remember have to do with doing things for her.' He gave them all a lazy smile. 'Now you all know what a monster of selfishness I am. I've been to a few weddings over the years, and the deal never appealed to me. In business you look after your own interests, and the other guy looks after his interests, and if you're me you end up with a lot of money and a lot of people who don't like you very much.'

There was another ripple of laughter.

'Now of course it's true that in the marriage ceremony you exchange vows, so if you promise to do everything you can to make the other person happy they promise to do the same for you. So if they do their part maybe you won't lose out too badly.' A black eyebrow slid up. 'On the other hand if you're as good as I am at looking after number one, why would you want to delegate?'

Someone said, 'Hear, hear.'

Chaz smiled. 'Quite.' He took a sip of wine. 'Well, it had me puzzled for years, why anyone would want to sign on for something like that.' He picked up the bottle of wine and filled Tasha's glass. 'Then I happened to remember a rather wet story I once read by O. Henry. The story is about a couple at Christmas. The gist of the story is that they don't have any money, but each has one precious thing. She has very long beautiful hair, and he has a gold watch. So she sells her hair to buy him a watch chain, and he sells his watch to buy her a tortoiseshell comb.

'You might think they both ended up losing out, because they'd each lost the one precious thing they had in the world. But what they actually had was something so rare you hardly ever come across it—they each wanted the other's happiness more than anything in the world. The hair and the watch were gone, but they still had that.'

He looked thoughtfully round the table. 'Well, it seemed to me that that was the point of marriage. You think you care about somebody's happiness more than you care about the gold watch, and you stand up in front of a lot of people and say so. Of course, you could be wrong—you could both be wrong; you could find you actually care more about the hair or the watch. But the idea of going into it making sure that, whatever happens, you're still going to have a gold watch at the end of the day strikes me as insane. If that was the thing I cared about most I wouldn't get married in the first place.'

Even in her rather depressed frame of mind, Tasha couldn't help being amused by the range of expressions around the table. These were people who'd been calling Chaz's girlfriends 'darling' for years because if you remembered a name from last time you could bet it was out of date. They'd been complaining of his restlessness, his refusal to settle down, his allergy to commitment. And now to be lectured on the meaning of marriage by the prodigal!

Chaz smiled at them benignly. 'Now, only a few hours ago I promised to do everything I could to make Tasha happy, so I obviously can't let you all make her miserable, and I can see it makes her miserable to think that marriage is all about hedging your bets. So I'd just like to go on record as saying that I disagree. It's a gamble—everything in life is a gamble. But in my opinion the thing you're playing for is the chance that you care about somebody else more than yourself. If you start out worrying about how to keep your watch safe, you've *already* lost the thing you were playing for; you've already decided you can't care about someone that much. Well, we may find we don't care about each other that way, and if so you can all say you told us so. But at least we'll have played for something worth winning. And after all, in the immortal words of someone or other, you can't win the lottery if you don't buy a ticket.'

There was scattered applause around the table. Tasha's father reached around her to grip Chaz's shoulder. Chaz's mother burst into tears.

'Oh, *darling*,' she sobbed into her handkerchief. 'I'm so happy for you. All these years I thought I'd ruined your life, I thought you couldn't love anybody, I thought you'd marry some society girl as a business accessory and never find true love.' She gulped. 'And now you're marrying dear little Tasha and you'll have children of your own. This is the happiest day of my life.' She burst into sobs again.

Chaz put an arm round his mother's shoulder and offered her a fresh handkerchief.

Tasha's mother said, 'Chaz, dear, that's a lovely, lovely thought, and I couldn't be more pleased that you feel that way. You *know* I've always thought of you as a son. I'm just saying that sometimes people have to be realistic.'

Chaz raised an eyebrow. 'And sometimes they can't afford to be. Shall we change the subject?'

Tasha's mother looked at him askance. Everyone in the family knew he had a razor-sharp tongue when provoked; he'd been uncharacteristically restrained today, but who knew how long that would last?

'Well, Chaz,' she said drily at last, 'if worse comes to worst at least I know you know *one* way to make her happy.'

'Exactly,' said Chaz. 'Protect her from her family. I don't remember making a vow on the subject, but I'll do my poor best.'

Tasha's father gave a crack of laughter.

Tasha's mother said, 'I *don't* think that's funny, Gervase.'

Local skirmishes broke out all around the table.

Tasha remembered suddenly just why she hadn't wanted to invite Chaz to her wedding in the first place.

They got through the rest of the dinner and the speeches somehow, and then their car took them to their hotel. Chaz had booked a suite at the Ritz, with a sitting room and two bedrooms. They were leaving the next morning for Paris.

They took the lift to their floor and were shown to the suite.

The door closed behind them, and they were alone.

'Alone at last,' said Chaz.

Tasha gave a rather tremulous smile. Chaz was surveying the suite and looking distinctly unimpressed, though to Tasha's eyes it looked palatial. When she didn't reply he glanced down at her. 'My poor darling,' he said ruefully. 'Your lovely wedding in ruins. Come here a minute.'

Tasha went wearily to his side. Considering that Chaz seemed to think sex was the solution for most of life's little problems she had a pretty good idea of what he had in mind, and she really wasn't in the mood either for sleeping with Chaz or for arguing with him about it, but she was too tired to argue that she wanted to stay where she was.

Chaz put his arms around her. At first she stiffened, thinking she should make sure he didn't get the wrong idea. His arms tightened, holding her close; she felt one hand stroking her hair. 'Poor Tash,' he said softly. 'All that trouble just to end up with Mr Wrong.'

Tasha giggled. The hours and hours of arguing over the guest list came back—the arguments over the style of invitation, arguments over refreshments, arguments over venue for reception, and after every argument all the work of putting it all into place. All that just so marriage-allergic Bad Cousin Chaz could walk in at the last minute and stroll down the aisle. Tasha thought of Chaz's look of horrified disbelief on first seeing the flower girls and she started giggling all over again. She remembered, vividly, Chaz's letter of refusal, her disgust at his rudeness, which was absolutely typical of the man, the way she'd shrugged and laughed because his absence was the one thing wanting to make the day perfect. And now her cheek was pressed against the jacket of the one person she'd wanted to stay away, because he'd come not to be just an unwelcome guest, but her husband.

She must have been out of her mind to agree to this, she thought. When Chaz had suggested it the pain of her disillusion with Jeremy had still been raw, so terrible it had made a kind of sense to think she must shield her father from it at all costs; and she'd been so tired that a whole year of being married to the wrong man had seemed a small price to pay to escape cancelling her invitations. If she'd had time to think about it she would never have done it, but she hadn't had the time—her father had come in about twenty minutes after they'd struck the deal, and Chaz had told him the news and then it had been too late.

Chaz was still holding her in his arms. 'I'd love to come,' his note had said, in the sneering tone she'd always hated; a simple no would have sufficed, but he'd had to go out of his way to be nasty. If she had to marry a substitute, why did it have to be someone who couldn't be in the room with her five minutes without getting under her skin?

Tasha looked at the disaster which was her life. It was so awful it was funny. She couldn't get a gold-digger, so she settled for someone she'd hated all her life. She started giggling uncontrollably, and suddenly the laughter turned into sobs, and she was sobbing her heart out on his chest.

'There, there,' said Chaz. He was still stroking her hair. 'Shhh. It'll be all right.'

Tasha kept sobbing. This was supposed to be the happiest day of her life. She'd met the right man and she'd been going to live happily ever after, and now what did she have to look forward to? A whole year with Chaz. Why, why, why, why had she said she'd do it? A flood of misery welled up inside her and burst its banks, pouring out in sobs over every bad thing that had ever happened to her. Every time she started to calm down she'd remember something else—the rabbit that had died when she was seven, or the time she'd tried to nurse a sick bird back to health and it had died. Everything went wrong. Nothing ever went right. Why couldn't she just die?

'All right,' said Chaz. 'All right.'

At last Tasha's sobs began to die down. There was something obscurely comforting in the strength of the arms around her, in the sheer solidity of the wall of his chest. She must have absolutely drenched his jacket, she thought dreamily.

And suddenly the enormity of what she'd done struck her. How *could* she do such a thing? She might not like Chaz, but how could she go into hysterics at being married to him when he was the one who was doing her a favour? She might not like him, but that didn't make it any better. Chaz had enough self-confidence for about five thousand other men put together, but he must have some feelings even if she'd never seen much sign of them—what on earth would it have been like for him to have had this storm of sobs?

She raised her face reluctantly. She hated to think what he'd think of her swollen, tear-blotched face, but she had to say something.

'Chaz, I'm so sorry,' she gulped.

Chaz was smiling down at her. His expression was probably the closest that sardonic, black-browed face could come to sympathetic.

'That's all right, Tash,' he said. An eyebrow quirked up ruefully. 'It was bound to hit you sooner or later.'

'Yes, but that was *terrible*,' said Tasha. She shouldn't let him go on holding her like this; it wasn't his job to cheer her up. Reluctantly she stepped back, and he dropped his arms. 'I mean, it wasn't because of you,' she said. It wasn't really true, but how could she not say it? You can't let someone get you out of a tight spot and then start crying because you don't like the rescuer.

'It's not really because of being married to you,' she said. 'It's just the whole thing. I thought I'd found the thing I wanted for the rest of my life, and now I don't have anything. I don't even know what I want now.'

She wiped her face with the back of her hand.

'Here, use this,' said Chaz, offering her a handkerchief. He smiled at her. 'It's sweet of you to try to spare my feelings, Tash, but if you'd gone looking for a substitute I doubt I'd have made the shortlist.'

'It was nice of you to offer,' said Tasha.

Chaz thrust his hands in his pockets, falling automatically into a loose-limbed, lazy stance which made her feel all the more clumsy and graceless.

'Tash, darling,' he said. 'This was my idea in the first place, remember? I know you were upset that night. You were in no state to weigh consequences. But I wasn't distraught; I knew perfectly well what I was doing.' He raised an eyebrow. 'Do you think I'd have suggested it if I thought we'd be at each other's throats for a year?'

'I don't know,' said Tasha. A smile tugged at her mouth. 'You always have the most extraordinary ideas, Chaz; you do things anyone else would consider completely outrageous.'

He laughed. 'Outrageous, yes, but I go out of my way to avoid boredom, and I can't imagine anything more boring than a year-long slanging match.' His eyes were bright with amusement. 'I know you don't like me very much, Tasha, but you don't actually know me very well. You know how bloody arrogant I am; well, I happen to think I improve on acquaintance.'

Tasha decided it would be more tactful not to reply to this. Her expression must have given her thoughts away, however; Chaz burst into laughter again.

'I don't expect you to agree, darling,' he grinned. 'But

just give it a chance. Once you get over the shock of the wedding I think you'll have a marvellous time.'

Tasha sighed. 'We'll see,' she said. Mention of the wedding suddenly reminded her of something. 'Chaz,' she said. 'I'm so stupid, I never even thought. Can you afford this? I mean can you really afford the time? How can you take a whole two weeks for a honeymoon when last week you said you couldn't even come to the wedding?'

Chaz gave her a gleaming glance. 'The first rule of business is to learn to prioritise, Tash. If I had the choice between going back to New York to water the office plants, and staying here to watch you sign yourself away to the unspeakable Jeremy, I'd be back on the first Concorde to deal with urgent office-plant-related issues.'

'I *thought* you'd made up all those excuses in your note,' said Tasha. 'It was the rudest thing I've ever seen in my life.'

Chaz laughed. 'Well, it was strictly intentional, darling. I suppose I wanted to convey my disapproval; I kept hoping against hope you'd have second thoughts.' An eyebrow flicked up. 'I suppose it's too much to hope Jeremy saw it?'

'*Yes,*' said Tasha. 'I just threw it away and crossed your name off the list.'

'Pity,' said Chaz. 'Still, he can't have been in any doubt of my opinion of him; that's one comfort.'

Chaz had met Jeremy the previous Christmas at her father's house, and had been outrageously, spectacularly rude. Even when Tasha had thought she was in love with Jeremy she had never thought verbal repartee one of his strengths; Jeremy had been completely unable to fend off the mercilessly witty barbs, and had retreated first into sullen resentment, and finally into an unexpected decision to go to his parents' house three days early. At the time Tasha had been furious with Chaz.

'No, I don't think so,' she said, suppressing a little smile.

'That's the spirit,' Chaz said approvingly. 'If you can't beat 'em, trounce 'em. Let's have some champagne.'

A bucket of ice with a chilled bottle stood by one of the sofas; glasses stood on the table. He opened the bottle and poured the golden foam into two glasses.

Tasha joined him by the sofa.

He handed her a glass, and raised his own. 'Cheers,' he said.

'Cheers,' said Tasha.

Chaz sank onto the sofa. Tasha sank down beside him; involuntarily she remembered the last time she'd sat on a sofa with him. She sipped her champagne, hoping he hadn't noticed her hot cheeks.

'It'll be all right, Tasha,' said Chaz, whose mind seemed for once to be preoccupied with something other than his main obsession. 'You're lucky you found out in time. One day you'll find the right man, and you can mean all those things you were saying today.'

'Do you really think so?' asked Tasha.

He flicked her hair with a casual finger. 'I'm sure of it.'

'Well, I hope you're right,' said Tasha. And then, because she thought they'd talked about her far too much already, she added, 'I hope you find the right woman, too.' She gave him a mischievous smile. 'If you did, would you say all those things and mean them? Or would she just be head of the harem?'

His eyes met hers. 'Would I forsake all others? Sure. If she was the right woman, why would I want anyone else?'

'Why do you do anything you do?' shrugged Tasha. 'I just wondered. Those things you said at dinner seemed so out of character.' She giggled. 'Did you see their faces? I don't think they could believe their ears. D'you remember that time you brought Veronica to lunch and Daddy kept calling her Julia? And then you brought Lucy to dinner just when I'd explained that you were seeing Veronica? And he called her Veronica and she said she wasn't Veronica and he said, "*Julia*. I didn't recognise you with that haircut. How nice to see you again!"'

'I remember. Well, you should be safe enough.'

One of her flyaway brows flickered upwards in an imitation of his own characteristic gesture. 'You know, I do think people were pretty tactless at the wedding,' she commented. 'Even if they *thought* it was a good thing you were turning over a new leaf, it was pretty rude to say it within your hearing. Some people even said it to your face! It's so patronising. How would you have felt if this had really been your wedding and all those people came up to lecture you? Frankly if you'd been rude back I think you'd have been completely justified.'

Chaz grinned. 'Well, thanks for that vote of support. But it's not their fault. I've done exactly as I pleased for years; naturally they think that's immoral.'

'Yes,' said Tasha. 'But it was your wedding day too. Who asked them to come and spoil it?'

Chaz twirled his glass in his hand for a moment, then glanced up at her. 'Tash, darling, if I met the right woman it would take more than a few moralising comments from dimly remembered aunts to spoil the day for me. I never gave a damn about them before; why should finding the one person in the world I did give a damn about make me any more interested in people I didn't want to see in the first place and could happily never see again? It was your idea to invite them.'

Tasha burst out laughing. 'Well, unfortunately it didn't occur to me to consult you when I was drawing up the guest list,' she sputtered. 'Naturally if I'd realised how you felt—' She thought of Chaz's reply to her invitation and burst out laughing again. 'Anyway,' she said encouragingly, 'today was just a fluke; it's sheer bad luck that my family is your family. If you do find the right person chances are she won't even be formally related to you, so you won't have to invite anyone you know. With any luck you'll never have to go through this again.'

Chaz was filling her glass again. 'With any luck,' he said, filling his own and putting down the bottle.

'What do you think she'd be like?' asked Tasha with genuine curiosity. She couldn't imagine what kind of woman would make her roving cousin Chaz decide to stop looking.

He considered a moment, then shrugged. 'I don't think I could come up with a checklist of what I was looking for, but I think I'd know it when I found it.'

'Have you ever thought you had?' Tasha asked impulsively, and then waited nervously for the reply. She knew only too well how brutally he could repulse people he thought were intruding on his private concerns. But it was so odd to be *alone* with Chaz—she didn't think she ever had been before that night last week, and for some reason it made him seem much more approachable.

He looked up at her over his glass. 'I thought I had, once.'

'But it didn't work out?' said Tasha.

He shrugged.

Tasha was staring at her cynical, sardonic sort-of cousin. What on earth would Chaz be like if he was in love? She just couldn't imagine it somehow. He'd always been such a Casanova. A thought occurred to her.

'Can I ask a question?' she said. 'I mean, you don't have to answer it if you don't want to, but if you don't want to could you just say you don't want to instead of using me for target practice?'

An eyebrow swooped up. 'That must be some question,' he said. 'Well, I'd better promise to be good; the suspense is killing me.' His eyes gleamed with mockery. 'What did you want to know?'

'Was it any different sleeping with someone you were in love with?' she asked.

'I don't know,' he said. 'Not a very interesting answer, but it's the best I can do. We never got that far.'

Tasha stared at him in wide-eyed disbelief. *Chaz* had actually been in love with somebody and he hadn't slept with her? 'You never slept together?' she said incredulously.

'No.'

'Why not?' she asked blankly.

'I didn't want to rush her.'

Tasha digested this in silence. It sounded completely out of character, but then maybe Chaz would act out of character if he was in love. She couldn't imagine what the girl could have been like, though. If she was in love with Chaz why wouldn't she want to sleep with him? Even Tasha, who'd never liked him, had never been blind to his good looks; why would someone who didn't see all his obvious faults not want to sleep with someone so impossibly handsome?

Then the answer came to her. It was blindingly obvious once she thought of it. The girl must have wanted to wait until she was married. Chaz had been madly in love and had wanted to respect her values and at the time had expected to marry her; he hadn't wanted to put her under any pressure. Then something had gone wrong and he hadn't married her after all.

Tasha's enormous mist-green eyes softened sympathetically. 'Do you ever regret it?' she asked.

'Sometimes.'

He emptied his glass and filled it again.

'You're very full of questions all of a sudden,' he remarked.

'Well, you said you wanted me to get to know you better,' Tasha pointed out.

He laughed. 'So I did.'

'I wonder if she ever regrets it,' Tasha remarked.

An eyebrow quirked up. 'It would be nice to think so.'

'She probably does,' said Tasha. For some reason she imagined the girl married to someone like Jeremy, looking back to the days when she had been in love with a man with kisses as smooth and golden and intoxicating as whisky, wondering what he would have been like.

'Well, here's hoping,' said Chaz. He stood up and stretched. 'Look, Tash, we've got to be up pretty early tomorrow to catch the train and it's been a long day. I think you'd better get to bed.'

Tasha stood up. She said shyly, 'I hope you didn't mind... I mean, I know it's none of my business.'

He smiled. 'Don't worry about it.' He bent and kissed her cheek. 'Goodnight, Tasha.'

Tasha realised irritably that she was actually disappointed. He could have kissed her goodnight properly. But she obviously couldn't kiss him or he might read all kinds of things into it.

'Goodnight, Chaz,' she said.

Chaz disappeared into his room. Tasha went into the vast room which had been set aside for her and changed into her nightgown.

It occurred to her suddenly that if everything had gone as planned she would have been undressing at this very moment for her wedding night with Jeremy.

Tasha laughed irrepressibly. She'd always respected her father's principles, but suddenly she felt a boundless affection for the education trust which was the main beneficiary of his wealth. But for that marvellous trust how rich and miserable she might have been! Now Jeremy had gone one way and she had gone another, and anything could happen.

She climbed into the enormous bed and fell into a deep and dreamless sleep.

Tasha woke up suddenly.

The room was bathed in moonlight; her alarm clock said 4:12.

It was perfectly silent.

She got out of bed and went to the door.

A lamp was on in the next room, its golden light throwing deep shadows across the hawk-like face of the man who was now her husband.

He was sitting with his legs up on the sofa, one knee drawn up, a book propped open on the knee.

Well, obviously if Chaz wanted to read a book at 4:12 in the morning he had every right to do so. Tasha hesitated, then walked forward barefooted across the carpet.

The nap of the carpet was so deep that she had reached the other end of the sofa before he heard her and looked up.

A shaft of moonlight silvered the pale cap of her hair. Her eyes, enormous in the pale face, were the dark shimmering green of a moonlit sea. Her white silk shift glimmered in the silver light.

'Natasha?' he said.

She came forward a few steps, sinking into the deep carpet. 'Chaz?' she said. 'Are you all right?'

He was wearing the bottom half of a pair of black silk pyjamas. Her eyes fell in spite of herself to the sleek, powerful shoulders, the taut belly and narrow waist, before meeting his eyes again.

'Of course,' he said. 'I couldn't sleep, so I thought I'd read for a while.'

'What are you reading?' asked Tasha.

'Spinoza,' he said. 'Present from your father.'

'I didn't know you were interested in Spinoza,' said Tasha, glancing at the book balanced on a powerful thigh.

'I'm not,' said Chaz. 'I was trying to get back to sleep.'

Tasha suppressed a smile at this heretical view. At least her father wasn't there to hear it.

'Well, I'll leave you to it,' she said.

'You only just got here,' said Chaz. His eyes were crackling with energy; no wonder he was having trouble sleeping. They fell in unashamed appreciation to the clinging white shift, then met hers again.

'Tasha?' said Chaz.

'Yes, Chaz?' said Tasha.

'I'd like to do something I know I'll regret.'

Tasha could feel her heart quickening at the look in his eyes.

'What's that?' she said huskily.

'Kiss you goodnight,' he said.

'Why?' said Tasha. 'Do you think it will help you sleep?'

'No,' said Chaz, 'I think it will put me well beyond the help of Spinoza, but what the hell? I've never been married before. I'd like to kiss my wife.'

Tasha laughed. She dropped to her knees beside him on the carpet, so that her face was level with his. 'Well, here I am,' she said softly. 'Do you want me to close my eyes?'

He shook his head. 'No, don't do that,' he said. 'They're so beautiful, I want to see them.' He put a hand in her hair, pulling her head gently towards him, and then his mouth found hers.

Her mouth opened to meet his, and it was as good as the last time, or maybe even better because last time she'd been so miserable. There was the same lovely smooth golden taste, with something wicked lurking just under the sweetness; she breathed in, savouring it, and her mouth curved in a smile because it was so lovely and she could feel his mouth curving against hers in an answering smile.

'Natasha,' he said, the smile warming his voice, and he kissed one corner of her mouth and then the other.

He raised his head, smiling into her eyes. She shivered involuntarily.

'You're cold!' exclaimed Chaz, all wide-eyed concern. 'Tash, darling, I'm a selfish swine. Here I am hogging the sofa while you sit on the floor.' He chucked the book unceremoniously to the floor and slid over onto his side. 'There you go,' he said, a glimmer of amusement in his eyes. 'Lots of room. Come up beside me before you catch your death.'

Tasha was half-tempted to remind him of all his assurances about no strings attached. But the kiss had been so lovely, and he looked lovely too, the long lean body stretched out the length of the sofa leaving room for her to join him.

'I'm sure this is a bad idea,' she said resignedly, getting up from her knees. She sank down onto the sofa and stretched out rather self-consciously beside him.

'But you were cold,' protested Chaz, all innocence. 'Come here and let me warm you.' He put an arm around her, holding her against him, and she could feel the warmth of his skin through the thin silk of her shift.

'Hello, Mrs Taggart,' he said, smiling into her eyes again. He kissed her, his arm tightening around her, and lifted his head. 'Is that better?' he said, the glimmer of amusement more pronounced. The unashamed desire in his eyes warmed her all the way down to her toes.

'Yes,' said Tasha. 'But I think this is a *very* bad idea.'

'Well, you know what they say—live dangerously.' He brushed her lips with his mouth.

'You always do,' said Tasha.

'Don't I know it,' he said wryly. His mouth found hers again, and he began kissing her with a leisurely expertise that turned her bones to water. She forgot about whether this was a good or bad idea; she forgot about making clear that it was just a kiss. Her body seemed to melt against his; her head seemed so dizzy she thought she would have fallen over if she hadn't been lying down. She lost track of time; all she knew was that the more he kissed her the more she wanted. Once he drew his head away, and without thinking she raised her hand to pull his head back down again, so that he laughed as his mouth met hers again; and once he raised his head and her mouth followed his hungrily while her arms closed round his neck, and he groaned and held her more tightly against him. Much, much later he raised his head again. She tried to kiss him again but he caught her head in his hand and held it away, looking into her eyes.

'Natasha,' he said very softly, and just watching his mouth frame the word she felt as if he were kissing her again. 'I haven't forgotten what I said. Do you want to hold me to it?'

She felt as if she were drowning in his eyes. It was as if her body were already part of his, as if nothing she could say could change that. She would melt around him and for the first time she would know what it was like to be one with someone. She'd never thought she would do this with someone she didn't love; it was strange how wrong it felt when after all they were married, and in the eyes of some people just that fact would make it right. But she couldn't argue, not even with herself; her body felt so different, as if it were doing something it had never done before.

'All right,' she said breathlessly, answering the question in his eyes rather than his words.

'All right?' he said.

'No,' said Tasha. 'I mean, yes. I mean—you know what I mean.'

'I think so,' he said. 'But are you sure you mean it?' His eyes were like great pools of black fire, waiting to engulf her. He was so beautiful—beautiful and terrifying. But maybe that was what it was supposed to be like.

'I'm sure,' she said.

He gave a laugh of pure happiness, his eyes alight. 'Tash, darling,' he said. 'God, you're beautiful.' He kissed her again, laughing. 'I promise I'll make it good for you, Mrs Taggart,' he said. 'I swear you won't regret it.'

Tasha smiled at him.

'I know,' she said. It felt wonderful to have the decision over and behind her. She breathed out on a long sigh. Then something occurred to her. 'Do you have anything we can use?' she asked.

'Do I—? I thought you were on the pill,' he said.

'I was,' said Tasha. 'I stopped taking it because I wasn't in a relationship. I thought there wasn't any point in taking it when I wouldn't be in a relationship for a year…'

There was something in his expression that made her uncomfortable, though she couldn't have said why.

'You said no strings attached,' she pointed out. 'I wasn't expecting to— That is, I thought you meant it, so I didn't expect to get involved with you.'

He laughed wryly. 'Of course you didn't,' he said. An eyebrow flicked up. 'No more did I, which is precisely why, I'm sorry to say, I don't have anything we can use.'

'Oh,' said Tasha. She swallowed. 'Well, maybe it wasn't such a good idea anyway,' she said.

He smiled, stroking her hair back with one finger. 'Could be. Felt like a good idea to me. God, you're lovely, Tash. Really lovely. You look so ethereal, but when you're in my arms you're like liquid fire—' He broke off, laughing. 'Oh God, I've made you blush. I'll stop talking before I really embarrass you.'

'It's just,' she said, 'you're so good at it. I'm not really used to it.'

'Good at it?' he raised an eyebrow.

'Your technique,' she said. 'It's really marvellous. I hadn't realised it made such a difference.'

'My technique,' said Chaz. 'Oh, yes. Well, glad you liked it.'

'And you *are* very handsome,' she said. She looked thoughtfully at the dark, hawk-like face; it was really amazing that someone so spectacular spared two minutes to look at her. 'Maybe that has something to do with it.'

'You don't have to analyse it to death, Tash,' Chaz said edgily.

For some reason he seemed rather annoyed. Suddenly Tasha realised what the problem was. He was frustrated. Of course, she was frustrated too, but people always said it was worse for men. Poor Chaz, and he was being so good about it too; *last* time he'd been absolutely furious.

'I'm sorry,' she said sympathetically. 'Would you like me to do something?'

'Do something?' Chaz said blankly.

'You know,' said Tasha. 'Do something else.'

Light dawned. 'Oh, my God,' said Chaz. He looked completely revolted. 'Why, so you can improve your technique?'

'Of course not,' said Tasha. 'I just thought—'

'I don't think I want to know what you thought,' said Chaz. 'Thanks, but no thanks.' He looked at her exasperatedly. 'For God's sake, Tash— Oh, never mind.' He shrugged.

Tasha ran a finger down the side of his face. Poor Chaz. 'You really are *very* good-looking,' she said.

A smile tugged at the corner of his mouth. 'And you're beautiful, Tash, but you'd try the patience of a saint and God knows I'm no saint. You'd better get off to bed before my beautiful technique breaks down into sheer brute raging lust.'

Tasha smiled at him. 'I hate to move,' she said truthfully.

'It's so lovely just lying here.' His body was so long and solid and muscular, its masculinity somehow disturbing and comforting at the same time. 'You've been awfully nice to me, Chaz,' she added, only half ironically. 'I thought you'd spend the whole time being horrible to me.'

A wry eyebrow flicked up. 'That's nothing to how nice I'd like to be to you, Tash,' he said. 'But something tells me we'd better call it a night.'

He gave her a sudden gleaming glance. 'Still, that doesn't mean we can't have one for the road.'

His head bent, and his mouth took possession of hers.

If he had given her time to reply she would have said that this was an even worse idea than the original suggestion; if she had been able to think, she would have thought that to invite further frustration was insane. She might have thought that she should hold back, for both their sakes, or just pull free and get off the sofa. If it had been like the times she'd kissed Jeremy it would have been perfectly easy to put together a sensible plan of this sort. She'd sometimes been embarrassed to discover, mid-kiss, that her mind was otherwise occupied: must pick up the dry cleaning, it would say. Almost out of toothpaste. Must remember to pay the gas bill. It would have been quite simple, in that sort of kiss, for her mind to throw up the helpful suggestion: must get off the sofa.

Unfortunately, from the point of view of making and carrying out sensible plans, this kiss was even worse, or from another point of view better, than the ones that had gone before. All the doubts and objections in her mind were blotted out. All the helpful little thoughts and suggestions that her mind had liked to present when she was kissing the man she loved were gone. Instead there was only sensation, as if his mouth, touching hers, had held a lighted match to a sheet of paper which in two seconds was a mass of flame.

Then suddenly he sat up, cursing softly. He was breathing fast; she could see his ribs moving with his quick shallow breaths.

She drew in a long shuddering breath. She couldn't speak; she could only look at his back. At last she forced herself up onto her elbows. He still hadn't turned to face her. She sat up, swinging her feet to the floor, and slid down the sofa to the end at his feet.

He gave her a rather mocking smile. 'Well, you know what I always say,' he said.

'What do you always say?' Tasha said faintly.

'Why settle for mildly frustrated when you can be wildly frustrated? Everything to excess, that's my motto.'

She would have liked to say something offhand too, but just looking at him made her hungry for him. It was infuriating. Why should he be able to make her feel this way? She didn't even like him. He was very good-looking, and there was no reason not to enjoy kissing him or even sleeping with him, if it had come to that. But why should he be able to make her want him so much it hurt?

He ran a hand through his hair, grimacing. 'I'm sorry, Tasha. Should have stopped when we were ahead. Still, you know what they say.'

'What do they say?' she said stupidly.

'A sorrow shared is a sorrow halved. We may suffer, but at least we don't suffer alone. Care to join me in a cold shower?'

Tasha realised that there were two things she would really like to do. The first was to hit Chaz. *Hard.* The second—worryingly, in view of the first—was to go to bed with him.

'No,' she said shortly.

He looked at her quizzically.

'Anyway, I don't believe you're suffering,' she said. 'If you were you wouldn't be making fun of me.'

He laughed, and even in her annoyance with him her eyes were drawn to the curve of his mouth. 'I'm not making fun of you,' he said. 'I'm just trying to see the humour in the situation. Has anyone ever told you you were like a stick of dynamite with a short fuse?'

'*No,*' snapped Tasha.

'Exactly. Because you've never come across the right man. And look at me. You're the first girl I've wanted to say it to. We're obviously meant for each other.'

'*What?*' said Tasha.

'On a physical level,' he said blandly. 'At the very least we've got the makings of an explosive affair. But for the lack of a little piece of plastic we could be blowing up the hotel. And instead, Tasha darling, we've signed on for a *mariage blanc*. It struck me as funny.'

Tasha recognised, resentfully, that there might be an element of truth in this. Otherwise why would her eyes be drinking in whatever they could see of an admittedly spectacular body? He was sitting with his legs drawn up, hands clasped around his knees; she could see the hard swell of his shoulders, the glimpses of the hard, lean belly. But—

Something struck her suddenly. 'But what about the girl?' she asked.

'What girl?'

'The one you were in love with,' she said. 'Wasn't it like this with her?'

He hesitated. 'I think I'd rather not talk about it, if you don't mind,' he said at last.

Well, it was better than some of the crushing snubs he'd delivered over the years.

He frowned slightly, obviously troubled by a painful memory. Then he flashed her a gleaming glance. 'Anyway, let's look on the bright side. We may not have gone all the way, but let's face it, half the way or even a quarter of the way with me has got to be better than going all the way with Jeremy. Imagine a whole lifetime of lying back and thinking of your laundry lists! What a lucky escape!'

The fact that Tasha had been thinking something perilously close to this did not reconcile her to hearing it from Chaz.

She stood up and glared at him. 'If you ask me,' she said, 'my only lucky escape was in not going to bed with *you*. Goodnight!'

She stalked out of the room.

# CHAPTER FOUR

TASHA woke up in the morning to brilliant sunshine. For a moment she did not know where she was. She looked in sleepy puzzlement at the luxurious room, a vague sense of excitement and anticipation bubbling up as if she were at the beginning of a holiday.

Then she remembered. This should have been the morning of her first day of married life with Jeremy. Instead she was waking up alone, about to embark on a honeymoon with Bad Cousin Chaz, and instead of crying herself to sleep and bursting into tears again as soon as she woke up, she was looking *forward* to it? Something must be wrong with her.

In fact, she thought, cheeks reddening, something must be seriously wrong with her. Not only had she not cried herself to sleep, she realised, but she had got up in the middle of the night and seriously considered going back to bed, this time with Bad Cousin Chaz. And now she was going to have to have breakfast with him.

Tasha leapt out of bed.

She opened her suitcase and scowled at it with crossed arms. She'd bought a few dresses to augment the jeans and T-shirts she usually wore when she wasn't at work; they'd seemed absolutely fine when the person who was going to see them was Jeremy. Now she held up first one dress and then another. She had a dark blue linen dress with a Nehru collar; it had looked pretty good in the fitting room. Or what about the sleeveless white silk with big black poppies? Or the pale green cotton?

There was a knock at the door.

'Tasha, do you want breakfast? We should be leaving in about half an hour.'

'I'm sorry,' said Tasha. 'I'm just trying to decide what to wear. I don't seem to have anything suitable.'

'Suitable for what? Eurostar doesn't have a dress code, Tash—it's strictly come as you are.' He sounded faintly amused.

'Suitable for not feeling a complete idiot,' Tasha muttered under her breath. She was standing in front of the full-length mirror, wearing the pale green dress, and holding up alternately the dark blue linen, the white silk with poppies and a canary-yellow dress that had looked fun in the shop but was now obviously a terrible, terrible mistake.

She met her eyes in the mirror. It was only too obvious what was going on. No prizes for working this one out.

Tasha could still remember the year she'd turned nine, the year before her parents' divorce. Her mother had gone on a diet and stuck to it for three months. She had bought an exercise bike and ridden it every day. She had bought new clothes and changed her hairstyle and spent hours changing her clothes and her make-up before catching the train up to London. It had only been much later that Tasha had understood the connection between this strange behaviour and the man who later became her mother's second husband. But once she'd understood she'd understood only too well. Everywhere she looked she'd seen grown-ups doing insane things because they were attracted to someone, regardless of the consequences for themselves or anyone else.

Well, this really was insane. She couldn't afford to get involved with Chaz. To be fair, he wasn't the type to come into her bedroom uninvited, or accidentally walk into the bathroom when she was taking a shower, but to be equally fair he most certainly was the type to make the most of any opportunities that offered. He was a born manipulator. He might not break the terms of their agreement first, but that wasn't to say he wouldn't do what he could to tempt her to set them aside. He probably found her a bit of a challenge—after all she'd been sticking pins in him for years.

She would simply have to make clear that she was sticking to the agreement and expected him to do the same.

No sooner had she reached this sensible decision than she seemed to hear his voice in her ear. 'I haven't forgotten what I said.' His eyes had been brilliant with desire, and yet at the time she'd been convinced he'd meant what he said. Well, maybe he had meant it in some sense, but he'd been safe enough asking. He'd kissed her senseless first, *then* he'd asked if she wanted to hold him to the agreement. Fine. She'd come to her senses again, and she was going to hold him to the agreement or know the reason why.

There was another knock.

'Tasha?'

'All *right*,' she said. She wasn't going to dress for him, that was for sure. She tossed the three dresses in her arms back in the suitcase, ripped off the pale green cotton and tossed it to a chair. She slipped into a dark olive green pullover, narrow-hipped white canvas jeans and dark green rope soled shoes. She bundled the last dress and her pyjamas into the suitcase, zipped it shut, and strode into the sitting room.

Chaz was standing beside the sofa, hands in his pockets, looking down at a newspaper. He was wearing a loose black jacket, black trousers and a charcoal-grey T-shirt. He looked, as always, as though he'd just been born with a sense of style and had never had to think about it. People said men were just as insecure about their looks and clothes as women, but the fact was, Tasha thought bitterly, that the men who were insecure were probably insecure because they didn't look like her abominable cousin.

He looked up as she came in the room, and smiled. In

spite of all her good intentions the smile was like a kick in
the solar plexus; the warmth in his eyes, the faintly rueful
curve of his mouth invited her to share regrets for the night
before—not for what *had* happened, of course, but for what
hadn't.

'Morning, Tash,' he said, strolling across the room. He
kissed her cheek and stood back. 'You look lovely,' he said,
still with that knee-weakening smile.

Tasha looked at him askance. She hadn't detected a note
of sarcasm; apparently he thought she looked lovely in an-
cient white jeans and a standard issue pullover.

'What, in this old thing?' she joked. 'I just threw on the
first thing I could find. I've had them for years.'

'Have you?' said Chaz, looking her up and down. 'Well,
you're still a sight for sore eyes. Must be love at last. Let's
have breakfast on the train, shall we? We're running a bit
late.' He picked up her suitcase and his own and headed
for the door.

Tasha bit her lip. If she didn't pluck up her courage now,
when would she? By the time they reached Paris all her
resolution might have melted away. Especially if Chaz kept
giving her smouldering looks the whole way.

'Chaz,' she said.

He stopped by the door. 'Yes?'

She came up to his side and forced herself to meet his
eyes.

'I just wanted to say, I've thought about it and I think
we should stick to our original agreement.'

'Fine.'

'We're going to be spending a year together,' she went
on. 'I think we should avoid potential causes of friction.'

Chaz gave a crack of laughter. 'Fine,' he said, his eyes
dancing. 'In that case we'd definitely better stick to the
plan.'

Tasha gritted her teeth. 'What happened last night was

perfectly understandable,' she said. 'But I think it was a bad idea and we should make sure it doesn't happen again.'

He was still smiling at her with that warmth in his eyes— it made her want to pull his head towards her and kiss him all over again, which was exactly what she wanted to avoid. But what was she supposed to do? She could hardly tell him to stop smiling.

'Tasha, darling,' he said, 'last night was lovely, but it was completely out of line. We agreed on the guidelines, and you came into this on that understanding. You'd have every right to be furious with me for setting them aside on the very first day.'

'Oh,' she said. Perversely, she wished he'd argue so she could argue back and put him in his place. What was she supposed to do when he agreed with her and kept smiling at her?

'It won't happen again. And now we really had better catch that train.'

The taxi swept them off down Piccadilly. The excitement Tasha had felt on waking up grew more acute. She had thought of the honeymoon only as adding plausibility to the wedding, but now it began to seem just the thing to take her mind off Jeremy. Too bad more people didn't go on honeymoons after being jilted, really.

Down Haymarket, across Trafalgar Square, up the Strand—but for Chaz she might have been trying to pick up the threads of her life, still travelling these streets every day, instead of mentally waving them goodbye.

The taxi shot across Waterloo Bridge. Hundreds of people were crossing the bridge on their way to work. She felt as if she were leaving the real hard world behind. Some day she would have to face it again, of course, but not just yet.

They got out at the International station, reaching the departure lounge with just minutes to spare.

Chaz had booked facing seats with a table. The first-class carriage was virtually empty—the only other travellers were a couple of businessmen at the far end who were already getting out their laptops.

Announcements were made in English and French. The doors shut. They were off.

An attendant came up with a choice of champagne or orange juice.

'Champagne,' Chaz said firmly.

The pale liquid bubbled up in the narrow glasses.

Chaz lifted his glass and touched it to hers.

'To us,' he said with a grin.

Tasha laughed. 'I think we need a sparkling champagne-type beverage for that toast,' she said. She shrugged. 'To us.' She took a sip and put down her glass.

The morning sunlight struck a flash of gold from her hand.

She turned the ring on her finger, shaking her head.

'We actually did this,' she said. 'I can't quite believe it.'

She reached impulsively across the table, and touched the gold ring on his finger.

'Real champagne,' she said. 'Real gold. You're really my husband. Does that feel odd?'

He took her hand in his for a moment, his thumb stroking the gold ring on her finger. Her hand tingled; she would have liked to snatch her hand back, but after all she'd started this.

'Very.' He grinned. 'If someone says Mrs Taggart I try to remember if my father has married anyone lately. I used to think people should specify the year—you know, treat it like the title to a beauty contest. Miss Universe 1997. Miss Universe 1998. Mrs Taggart 1999. Jane is the holder of the Mrs Taggart title for four straight years. The record for the

longest holder of the title is still held by the first Mrs
Taggart, Louise, who saw off all contenders for an unpar-
alleled seven years. Louise, Mrs Taggart '68, '69, '70, '71,
'72, '73 and '74 has nothing but praise for more recent
champions. "The game is a lot tougher than it was in my
day," she says. "I don't know how they put up with it. He
was never what you'd call an easy man to live with, but
the way he is now I wouldn't last two seconds."'

His thumb was still sliding back and forth over the narrow band of gold. He raised an amused eyebrow. 'I sort of
feel as if I'm setting up a rival Miss Universe contest, introducing a new Mrs Taggart to the world.'

'You mean it's really no big deal,' said Tasha.

He shrugged. 'We wear these two little pieces of metal
that say I belong to you and you belong to me. It might be
a big deal if that were true, but we both know it's not. The
fact that you're wearing that piece of metal on your finger
doesn't mean I have any rights over you.'

'Legally you do,' said Tasha.

'Not very interesting ones,' he said flippantly. He put her
hand down, finished his glass of champagne and set it down
with a click. That unsettling, smiling look was back in his
eyes. 'Now if only this ring were like a piece of mistletoe,'
he said, 'I could kiss you as long as you had it on.
Unfortunately it doesn't work that way.'

'Last night you thought it did,' she blurted out.

'Last night,' he said, 'I kept feeling that just the words
"my wife" were like a piece of mistletoe, only of course
they weren't. That was why I spent the better part of my
wedding night getting to know Spinoza.' A smile tugged
at the corner of his mouth. 'It's true, of course, that when
you came in the idea of having a wife and kissing her
seemed pretty compelling—but on the other hand, you
know, I did ask. If just wearing the ring made such a difference seems to me I could have assumed the answer was

yes, at least on day one. Whereas in fact we've just agreed I should assume the answer is no.'

Tasha flushed. If only she could take back that stupid reference to last night! Well, at least she could make sure the agreement was well and truly in place.

'Yes,' she said emphatically. 'That's exactly right.'

The look of amused comprehension in his eyes was not at all what she was aiming for. He raised a quizzical eye-brow. 'Of course, I *can* call you Mrs Taggart whenever the mood strikes me. Can't say it exactly sets the pulse racing.' He appeared to pause for thought. 'Then again, I could call you Mrs Taggart and just think of all the things I'd like to do under the mistletoe.'

'Don't you *dare*!'

'Call you Mrs Taggart?' His eyes were dancing.

'You know perfectly well what I mean,' she snapped.

'Tasha, darling, I'll do my level best to be pure in deed, but I really can't answer for my thoughts.' He grinned. 'If it really bothers you, though, I'll try not to call you Mrs Taggart when I'm thinking about what might have been. At least then you won't have to know I'm thinking it.'

Tasha drank off the rest of her champagne at a single swallow. This was *hopeless*, she thought furiously. What was the use of insisting he keep his hands to himself if he was going to flirt with her unmercifully for the rest of the year?

'Maybe we should see if we can find some breakfast,' she said. 'I shouldn't really be drinking this on an empty stomach.'

'All right, Mrs Taggart,' said Chaz. 'Whatever you say.'

They reached the Gare du Nord just before lunch. Chaz found a taxi outside the station, and soon Tasha found her-self standing on the pavement in front of a charming old-fashioned hotel on the Left Bank.

'It's a little basic,' said Chaz. 'But I like the atmosphere. I always thought it would be just the place for a honeymoon. See what you think.'

They were shown up to a suite of three rooms on the first floor. What Tasha thought was that if this was his idea of basic, she shuddered to think what he'd make of the sort of place she usually stayed. In fact, she shuddered to think what a hotel would have to come up with to rank as better than basic. Her father had always lived very simply, however much money he had, and had encouraged his children to do the same—it had been one of the major points of disagreement with her mother, who liked her comforts. Well, this spectacular room would certainly have met with her mother's approval.

The walls were of white plaster, the ceiling of white plaster with wooden beams showing, and within this simple frame the room was ablaze with colour. The floor was covered with brilliantly coloured kilims. The bed was a kind of enormous divan strewn with cushions. An elaborately carved Moroccan screen in gleaming black wood stood by a real fireplace tiled with blue and white tiles. And everywhere she looked was a profusion of beautiful plants—a Madagascar palm in a pot with a glowing red crackle glaze in one corner, two lemon trees with glossy dark green leaves flanking the window...

The bell boy put Tasha's suitcase on a rack which would allow her to open it and unpack without lifting it. He then hefted Chaz's suitcase next door. The sound of enthusiastic French came muffled through the door, presumably in response to an unexpectedly generous token of appreciation.

Chaz came through the door of the connecting bathroom. 'Well?'

'It's beautiful,' said Tasha. 'Have you stayed here often?'

'No, never.' He was looking out the window into the courtyard. 'A couple of friends from Rome always stay here when they're in Paris. Teresa tends to run anything from half an hour to three hours late, so if I'm meeting them I usually come up to the room and talk to Guido. Always thought I'd like to stay here. It seemed a shame to waste it on a business trip, though—thought I'd save it for something special.'

'Oh,' said Tasha. 'Well, I'm glad you thought this counted. It's really lovely.'

'Glad you like it.' He turned to face her. 'What would you like to do now?' he asked.

'I hadn't really thought,' said Tasha. 'I suppose I could unpack.' She hesitated. 'What are your plans?'

'My plans?'

'I don't want to get in your way if there are things you have to do,' she said. 'It was wonderful of you to arrange this, just as if it was a genuine honeymoon—it will make it much easier when I talk about it to Daddy and people. But you don't have to spend all your time with me. There's so much to see here, I'm sure I can find plenty to occupy myself, and after all you've seen it all before. You won't want to go trekking around the Louvre with me.'

'You'd like to see the Louvre?' he said. Tasha couldn't quite make out his expression.

'And all the other things,' she agreed. 'I'm sure you wouldn't be seen dead in the Eiffel Tower, Chaz—I can't go dragging you along just because *I've* always had a hankering to see it.' She laughed. 'It's hard to believe I've never been here before. I've always wanted to, ever since I was a little girl.'

She crossed the room to stand by him, looking out the window. 'There's something so romantic about Paris, isn't there?' she said dreamily. 'You feel anything could happen.'

'Do you?' said Chaz drily.

'Mmm,' said Tasha.

'Well, obviously do whatever you want,' said Chaz. 'If you'd like company let me know; if you'd like to go off on your own that's fine. There's a TV company I've been thinking of investing in—I could use the chance to talk to some people.'

Tasha looked at him doubtfully. It almost sounded as if he'd assumed they'd be going around together. But that was absurd. It wasn't as if they had anything in common, after all. They'd agreed to go ahead with the honeymoon to add credibility to the wedding—if they'd instantly flown back to New York they might have fooled some people, but never her father.

She was about to say that of course he was welcome if he *wanted* to come, when a thought struck her. There were a lot of things she did not really understand about Chaz's reasons for suggesting this. She'd been so desperate that she'd accepted his assurances that there was no hidden agenda. The further that stormy night at her father's retreated into the past, however, the stranger the whole thing looked. As Chaz himself had said, *she* might have been distraught, but he certainly hadn't. Well, she would never have agreed to it in a million years if she *hadn't* been distraught. If Chaz, in full possession of his senses, had come up with the idea, there had to be a lot more going on than met the eye.

Well, he obviously wasn't after her money. What else he might have in mind she couldn't imagine, but she didn't want any part of it. She just wanted to get her life back on track. She would put in the necessary two weeks in Paris to convince everyone it was a genuine marriage, then she'd go to New York with Chaz and look for some new direction for her life.

Tasha frowned. Chaz could be charming enough when he wanted; it turned out he could even be sympathetic when he chose. In her present state of mind she knew she was vulnerable; she'd already seen how natural it had seemed to turn to him. What that showed was not that she'd mis-judged him, but that she was much, much more vulnerable than she'd suspected. Maybe her self-esteem had been wounded more than she'd thought by being jilted—it was certainly flattering to have Chaz pay her attention. Or maybe she was so lonely and isolated that *any* sympathy looked like proof of a warm, caring personality. But the fact was, dangerous though it might be to have a purely physical relationship with Chaz, it would be a million times more dangerous to risk any kind of emotional dependency. For years, when she *hadn't* been completely devastated, she'd had an extremely clear-eyed view of her handsome, selfish cousin. Now was emphatically *not* the time to be revising her opinion. It was *not* the time to be making her-self vulnerable all over again.

Fine. She would just ignore all the undercurrents in the conversation.

'That sounds like a good idea,' Tasha said blandly. 'If you've been thinking of investing in this company, it could be a blessing in disguise that you've ended up visiting Paris just now. You can talk to some people, and I can go sight-seeing.'

'Then that's that taken care of,' said Chaz.

There *was* something going on, thought Tasha, taking in his carefully offhand tone of voice. She *knew* she hadn't imagined it.

'You know, you really don't have to keep pretending to be my husband,' she said. 'I don't want to interfere with your usual social life. I'm sure if you were here on your own you'd look up some of your old girlfriends, or maybe try to find a new one.'

Chaz was suddenly very still.

'We've got separate rooms, after all,' she went on.

'There's no reason why you shouldn't do whatever you'd usually do.'

If she'd wanted to, she could have counted the seconds until he answered. For what seemed an interminable moment the only sound in the room was the soft ticking of the watch on her wrist.

'That's very thoughtful of you, Tash,' he said drily at last.

He took her chin in his hand and held it, forcing her eyes to meet his.

'If you'd rather spend time alone, that's fine,' he said. 'If you don't want to sleep with me, that's fine too. But all you have to do is say so. You don't have to provide alternative arrangements.'

'That's not what I meant—'

'Isn't it?' The black eyes bored into hers. 'I know you don't like being attracted to me,' he said coolly. 'You know I'm not going to force myself on you, but that's not exactly the problem. The problem is, if you change your mind you can't go on counting on me to protect you from yourself. You'd feel safer if you knew another woman was in my bed.'

'That's not true!' Tasha said hotly.

A black eyebrow shot up in the exaggerated mockery she'd always hated. 'Think you'd be tempted to join us, Tash? Now that I never would have guessed—'

'You know that's not what I meant!'

'No?' The lazy voice mocked her.

Tasha jerked her head back, trying to free her chin. His grip tightened. She took his wrist in her hand and pulled it aside—and then, because there was no reason to think he wouldn't take hold of her again when his hand was free, she found herself stuck gripping his wrist. The palm of her hand tingled as if an electric current ran through the warm skin of his arm.

Chaz smiled. He raised his other hand. Tasha grabbed his wrist, glaring at him. He surrendered it without a struggle, and somehow she now found herself standing foursquare to him, holding his wrists.

He glanced down and laughed. 'Tash, darling,' he said, and for some reason the acid edge to his voice was gone again. 'I know that's not what you meant.'

'And I don't know why you make such a big deal of it,' she added. 'I'm only saying pretty much what you said yourself the other day. You said you were going to sleep with other women and everyone would understand when we got a divorce. What difference does it make when you start?'

He did not reply at first. He lowered his hands; Tasha continued to hold his wrists as a precaution. Then he moved his hands behind his back, so that she was drawn up against him. She was as close to him as she had been the night before. His face was bent down towards her; she could smell the faint scent of his aftershave.

'It's not a question of what you said,' said Chaz. 'It's a question of why you said it.' His eyebrow flickered up. 'You don't actually have to go on holding me, you know.'

Tasha dropped her hands and stepped back, watching him suspiciously. He put his hands in his pockets.

'I know you've got a lot on your mind,' he said. 'You tell me you'd like to stick by our original agreement. Fine. What do you want me to say? That even if you change your mind I'll tell you I'm not interested? But I'd be absolutely delighted if you changed your mind. Do you want me to say it's a bad idea? I've no idea whether it's a bad idea or not. I don't find the possibility of enjoying sex as dangerous as you seem to; I don't actually know whether that's because I'm more experienced, or because you know something about yourself that I don't know. It's your call, anyway, and I'm prepared to respect that.'

A lock of black hair had fallen forward into his face, giving him a slightly boyish look. He said ruefully, 'But that's not enough for you; you'd like some better guarantee. You want to put a lot of safeguards in place that will make it absolutely certain not only that you don't sleep with someone when you think you shouldn't, but also that you have as boring a time as possible in one of the most wonderful cities in the world. I've always thought the phrase ''clean fun'' one of the most repulsive in the language, but let's just say we could have a pretty good time here without taking off any of our clothes—instead you'd like to spend your days dutifully going round museums looking at things someone else said you should see, and your nights imagining what's going on in another room.'

Tasha glared at him, searching for the retort that would pulverise him. Suddenly a thought struck her. It's not what you say, it's why you say it... Why had Chaz wasted all this eloquence on blasting her out of the water for something he'd suggested himself?

Something strange *was* going on.

In two seconds an answer of sorts had come to her. Maybe there had been an element of altruism in Chaz's proposal, and maybe he really had meant there were no strings attached. But all men were capable of amazing feats of doublethink when it came to sex, and Chaz was anything but the exception to the rule. As far as he was concerned, she was a piece of unfinished business.

As long as she remained unfinished business, he was just going to go on flirting and being as charming as he knew how. Next thing she knew she'd find herself swept into a 'Paris in the Springtime Experience', romantically kissing Chaz under a full moon on the Pont Neuf. One thing would lead to another. Then she'd have a whole year in New York as yet another piece of finished business.

Well, she wasn't having any of it. She wanted to put her

stay in New York to good account. She wanted to get her life back on track.

Telling Chaz to leave her alone was obviously not going to work. But if there was one thing Chaz hated, it was being bored.

Well, when in doubt use your enemy's weight against him.

'Why, Chaz,' she said. 'I'm sorry you think going to museums such a waste of time. But if you'd *like* to visit the Louvre with me you're very welcome. You should have said.'

# CHAPTER FIVE

THEY had lunch at a small bistro near the hotel. Tasha then insisted on going to the English-language bookshop on the Rue de Rivoli to pick up some guidebooks. She hadn't had a chance in the rush before the wedding, she explained. She just wanted to make the most of her time in Paris.

The shop naturally had a large selection of books on France, Paris and the treasures of the Louvre. She took one off the shelf and turned to the Louvre.

'The immense size of the collection can be intimidating on a first visit,' said the guide. 'You can't see everything and shouldn't try to.'

Well, what did they know? Tasha tucked the book under her elbow and pulled another off the shelf.

This one explained that the Louvre contained some thirty thousand works of art. Excellent! Apparently it could take as much as thirty minutes just to leave your bag and coat at the cloakroom! Better and better! The book added that you should not try to see everything and that you should think about leaving your coat at home. Leave her coat at home? When Chaz could spend a solid half-hour standing in a queue? That would never do! She tucked it under her arm and continued to browse.

Most guidebooks tried to cater to a range of travellers: people with different budgets, people with more or less time at their disposal. The problem was, there really wasn't a guidebook aimed at the newlywed who has come to Paris on her honeymoon and wants to spend as little time as possible with her husband. All the books were keen to help you be selective, when Tasha wanted an excuse to see every single one of the paintings, sculptures, tapestries, mummies, screens, fans, vases, clocks and miscellaneous items which filled the former palace.

She didn't know what Chaz was up to, but whatever whim had possessed him to take an interest in her was not going to stand up to a solid week in the Louvre. She wouldn't have him begging for mercy by the end of the week, but she'd have him suddenly remembering some friends he wanted to see. Or if a week wasn't enough, good heavens, there were a couple of other museums right at the other end of the Jardin des Tuileries. And if those didn't do the trick, Paris was absolutely crammed with the sort of places everyone knows you should visit selectively, choosing what you want to see, not trying to see everything...

She bought the two guidebooks, and a book on art treasures of the Louvre. This would have to do.

'I thought we could just look at the Assyrian and Egyptian departments today,' she informed Chaz, as they walked back down the Jardin des Tuileries to the museum. 'After all we're already well into the afternoon; we may as well be realistic about what we can expect to see.'

'Fine,' said Chaz.

'Then we can come back tomorrow and really get our teeth into it,' she said cheerfully.

'Fine,' said Chaz.

They walked into the glass pyramid to buy their tickets. There wasn't much of a queue—well, better luck tomorrow morning. Then they walked over to the museum proper, along with streams of other tourists.

Before they could go in, of course, they had to go through security clearance.

'Oh, dear, there seems to be rather a long queue,' Tasha commented, trying to sound disappointed. Something in Chaz's expression suggested she had not succeeded.

They finally made their way downstairs to the Assyrian

collection. Tasha insisted on looking at every single object
there with frequent references to her three guidebooks.
When the object was mentioned she would read out items
of interest. When it wasn't mentioned she would look in
the other guidebooks. Under other circumstances she would
have been impressed by the extraordinary collection; today
she was too busy persuading Chaz he would be happier
elsewhere.

It wasn't easy to tell how well she was doing. Chaz
strolled around, hands thrust in his pockets, responding oc-
casionally to the snippets of information she doled out. He
didn't seem desperately bored yet. Well, it was early days.

The museum closed at six.

'Oh, what a shame,' lamented Tasha. 'I was hoping we
could squeeze in that room of Islamic tiles, but the time
just slipped away somehow.'

Chaz grinned. 'Well, tomorrow is another day,' he said.
'Why don't we find a café and have an aperitif?'

Tasha was prepared for this. 'Oh, I think I'd rather see
Notre Dame,' she said promptly. 'There's plenty of time
before dinner. But of course if *you'd* like to have an aperitif
you don't have to come.'

His grin broadened. 'Of course I'll come,' he said. 'I
wouldn't miss it for worlds.'

The days that followed fell into a pattern. At Tasha's insistence they would get up early so as to be at the museum
the moment it opened. They would have croissants and big
cups of milky coffee at a local café, then go to the Louvre
where Tasha, armed with her guidebooks, would proceed
through the galleries painting by painting. After hours she
followed a similar plan in various notable churches. On
Tuesday, when the Louvre was closed, she took him to the
cemetery at Père Lachaise to look at famous graves tombstone by tombstone.

Somehow nothing seemed to go according to plan.

No one could possibly know about everything they saw, but Chaz knew an unnerving amount about things that could be summed up as sex and money. He seemed to have an encyclopaedic knowledge of political and amorous machinations through the ages, and entertained her with a cynical commentary on artists, patrons and their love interests. Tasha invariably ended up getting in an argument with him. Chaz would stand there, hands in his pockets, smiling lazily down at her until she lost her train of thought and came stammering to a halt—only to discover that they had an audience. Chaz could beat the other tour guides hands down, if not for aesthetic appreciation than for good looks and sheer narrative verve, and a steady stream of defectors from other tours tended to gather round. So did independent visitors who had previously thought they didn't want a guide.

The advantage to the plan was supposed to be that she could spend the whole day with Chaz without even looking at him. But it wasn't really possible to avoid looking at him. And even when she wasn't looking at him she was uncomfortably, cracklingly aware of him. It was as if there were a magnetic field between them, something she had to resist standing by him. He was supposed to be the one maddened to frenzy; instead she found she was getting more and more irritable.

The museum was simply not boring him as much as it was supposed to. And besides she still had to look at and talk to him at breakfast, lunch and dinner. She tried to keep those under control by talking non-stop about what they'd just seen or what she was planning to see next. You'd have thought it would quickly have discouraged him from spending meals with her, but no such luck. He just sat there making suspiciously polite conversation, with an amused look in his eyes that made her want to hit him.

After dinner Chaz would ask if she'd like to go to a club, and Tasha would explain that she was rather tired and she thought she would just go back to the hotel and go to bed, but of course if *he* wanted to go to a club that was absolutely fine. Chaz would protest, with another amused look, that he wouldn't dream of it. So they would go back to the hotel together. Chaz would kiss her on the cheek and say goodnight and go into his room.

Maybe he went to sleep straight away, or maybe he stayed up reading Spinoza—Tasha was often awake until three or four in the morning, but she stayed in her own bed staring into the dark. And that would be another day when she had not got involved with Bad Cousin Chaz.

It didn't help that the better she got to know him the more inadequate she felt.

One morning at breakfast she made the mistake of asking him about his work.

'What will you do when you get back to New York?' asked Tasha. 'Is somebody else looking after—well, whatever it is you do?'

'I'm between projects at the moment,' he said. 'So we're actually in a pretty similar situation—I've been trying to decide what next.'

'And what exactly do you do?' asked Tasha. Extravagant rumours floated around the family, but the only thing she really knew about Chaz was that he kept making money.

'Well, I do pretty much whatever appeals to me.' He grinned. 'As you probably know, I struck it lucky with a couple of musicals in the West End a few years back. It was fun while it lasted, but I didn't want to do another, so I took some of the money and started a club in New York. Much more exciting than musicals—you know, you're giving their first chance to the bands that everyone else will be raving about in a year or two—but once it was a success it got so it was just routine, so I sold out. Then I thought it would be fun to produce a film—that's when I got together with Dave Kramer and we came up with *Chameleon*.

'I spent a while building up the production company,' he went on. 'Again, it was fun while it lasted, but I thought it was time to move on. I sold it to one of the majors a few months ago. I was thinking of buying a radio station—there was one that looked quite attractive that I'd heard might be disposed of. Then I…' He hesitated briefly. 'Then I decided not to. So I'm trying to make up my mind what to do instead.'

'Oh,' said Tasha, impressed and depressed in spite of herself.

He caught the odd note in her voice. 'What is it?' he asked.

'Nothing,' said Tasha.

Chaz gave her one of the smiling looks which she'd been unable to stamp out after five solid days of the glories of art. Night after night she'd think he'd have to give up at last, only to find another of those smiles sizzling across the breakfast table next day. 'Doesn't sound like nothing to me,' he said.

Tasha shrugged. 'I don't know,' she said. 'I keep switching track too, but I can't say *I* ever end up with a lot of money. Everything always ends in disaster and then I just pick up the pieces and try something else.'

'That's not really true, though, is it?' said Chaz.

'Of course it's true. My finals were a disaster, my first job was a disaster, my second job was a disaster—and every single relationship I've had has been a disaster too.'

Chaz raised an eyebrow. 'But the two aren't exactly unconnected, are they? You're always complaining about how selfish I am. Well, if you singlemindedly do exactly what you want to do you stand to make a success of it. I've never been involved with anyone to an extent that would interfere with whatever I was working on at the time.'

'Hmm,' said Tasha. It was true that the men she'd gone out with had all assumed that if you loved them you would give up everything else you cared about. At the same time she couldn't help feeling stupid and inadequate. Even if she'd gone the route of disposable boyfriends, she doubted she'd ever have made a success of four or five careers in quick succession. And now what was she going to do? She'd wanted to get away from London, where she knew too many people, where she'd feel everyone was talking about her. But in New York, of course, she wouldn't have any contacts. What was she going to do?

'I'll introduce you to some people when we get to New York,' said Chaz, as if reading her mind. 'Maybe you'll find something that appeals to you. I met Peter McDermott once—didn't he work with you at Dufferins Press? He said you were very talented and could do pretty much anything you set your mind to; it was just too bad you'd set it to producing a book by a talentless idiot.'

Tasha gritted her teeth. She knew she should be grateful. She supposed she shouldn't grudge Chaz his success. In fact, she should probably apologise, at least mentally, for a lot of things she'd thought of him over the years. She'd always thought he was nothing but an opportunist, that he had a spectacular talent for making money because it was the only thing that interested him.

'Thank you,' she forced herself to say.

'My pleasure,' said Chaz. His mouth quirked in a smile. 'And now we'd better get going if we're to be there when the doors open.'

Tasha sat up in bed, arms clasped round her knees, scowling into the dark. They'd seen thousands of works of art and Chaz showed no sign of weakening. Churches hadn't worked. Neither had the cemetery. She was beginning to think she had started with the wrong kind of sight.

She turned on her bedside lamp and looked through the back of her guidebook. Obviously some museums had a broader appeal than others. It was just a matter of finding a museum so boring Chaz would give in at last.

She knew exactly what she wanted: the type of museum that had a couple of dusty old spinning wheels with a wax model of a woman in a mob cap, *plus* a display of buttons through the ages, *plus* a display of moths and a stuffed newt. Britain, of course, was abundantly supplied with museums of this type—they existed to send business to the local pub. Would France, with no tradition of local pubs to support, have such a museum? Would Paris? The problem with the Louvre, obviously, was that it was just too good.

Tasha started flipping through the pages. There were a lot of museums listed, but they sounded pretty interesting. Maybe the guide had left out the boring ones—

Tasha froze. The light had gone on in the connecting bathroom. She could see the narrow band of light under the door.

The shower started up.

She flicked through the pages of her book, trying to concentrate.

The sound of the falling water muted suddenly as he stepped under it. She had a vivid image of the water pouring down over his hair and face, his head the sleek silky black of a seal under the silver jets, of water sliding down over gleaming shoulders, down the broad chest, down the hard, flat stomach, down... In her imagination she saw the whole of the long, lean body turning under the hard spray, slick with the water that streamed down to pool at his feet...

His amused voice came to her mind. 'What do you want me to say? That even if you change your mind I'll tell you I'm not interested? But I'd be absolutely delighted if you changed your mind.' He hadn't locked the door. He'd be absolutely delighted if she walked straight in…

She turned another page of her guidebook. She wondered, suddenly, what would happen if she did walk in. Was he assuming she would before the honeymoon was over? They'd been in Paris six days. Maybe he'd already bought contraceptives.

She was scowling at the thought when the phone rang on her bedside table.

Tasha picked it up. 'Er, *oui*?' she said.

*'Monsieur Taggart est là? C'est très urgent.'*

Tasha worked out, after a moment, that the operator thought Mr Taggart might be there and that it was urgent. She was about to ask indignantly why they thought Mr Taggart would be in her bedroom at this time of night when she remembered that she was Mrs Taggart.

'Er,' she said. *'Un moment.'*

But before she could call Chaz a man's voice came down the line.

'Chaz!' exclaimed an American voice. 'Jack here, look I hate to barge in on your honeymoon but this can't wait. I just heard that the WQBQ deal is stalling. There's a chance to get in there if you move fast—'

Tasha tried to stop the flow.

'I'm sorry, Chaz is in the shower,' she said. 'The operator put the call through before I could get him.'

*'Oh,'* said the voice. 'You must be Natasha! This is Jack Vale. Chaz and I go back a long way. Pleased to meet you. Sorry to butt in like this, but he really can't afford not to know—'

'I'll just get him now,' said Tasha.

She went to the bathroom door and knocked.

'Chaz?'

'Yes?'

'A phone call for you,' she said. 'Jack Vale. He says it can't wait.'

'Right. Tell him I'll be there in just a minute.'

Tasha returned to the phone.

'He'll be here in just a minute,' she said. She smoothed up her covers and sat cross-legged on the bed. She was wearing a long T-shirt tonight, which wasn't exactly suggestive.

'Great.' There was a short pause. 'So how are you guys enjoying Paris?' he asked.

'Very much,' said Tasha.

'I'll *bet* you are,' said Jack. 'Paris in the spring…'

Tasha missed whatever followed, because the bathroom door had opened.

Chaz had apparently dried himself in a cursory way. His chest was still damp, his hair slicked back, and he had knotted the damp towel around his hips. He walked quickly towards her, his bare feet leaving damp footprints on the carpet.

He picked up the phone. 'Jack?'

There was a short pause.

'No, that's fine, don't worry about it. What seems to be the problem?'

There was another, longer pause. He glanced at Tasha.

'Do you want me to leave?' she whispered.

He shook his head.

'The deal fell through?' he was saying. 'Oh—so nothing definite—oh, I see. Right. Yes. Yes, that's very interesting.'

He sat down on the bed beside her, his dark face intent. Little beads of moisture were trickling down the dark hair on his chest, down the line of dark hair that traced its way to the towel. 'Right,' he said. 'Sure.' He was sitting on a corner of her book, the cloth of the towel pulled tight along the hard line of his thigh. She wished she could look away. The ends of the towel had fallen loose on either side of his

other thigh, which was bare almost all the way to the hip...
'Fine,' said Chaz.

Finally Chaz said, 'Look, Jack, thanks for calling, but I
can't see my way to doing anything about it. Yes, I do
realise that—no—no—sorry, Jack, but that's my final word.
I'll talk to you when I get back.'

He hung up.

Tasha said, 'Is that the radio station you were telling me
about? Are you *sure* you don't want it? Maybe we should
just go back to New York.'

He smiled at her. 'What, and miss all the fun here?'

'But your friend seemed to think you still wanted it,'
said Tasha.

'People always think they know what you want better
than you do yourself,' said Chaz. 'Jack means well, but I'd
made up my mind not to go ahead with it.'

'Oh,' said Tasha.

He shifted his weight slightly, releasing her book.

'And what have we here?' he asked, picking it up. 'De-
ciding what to do tomorrow?'

'I was thinking of looking at a few other museums,' said
Tasha.

'Not tired of the Louvre already!' exclaimed Chaz.
'Well, we can always go back. Let's see, what else can we
try?'

He slid further over onto the bed, propping himself on
an elbow, and began flipping through the book. 'Hmm,
there's the Impressionists at the Orangerie, of course, but
*everyone* sees those; maybe we could find something a little
more out of the way. A button museum. Gloves of France
through the Ages...'

'Are you sure you don't want to go back to New York,'
Tasha persevered. Her eyes were devouring the long, lazy
line of his body, the muscle of his arm flexed to support

his weight... If only they were back in New York, with Chaz working twenty hours a day on this radio station!

He looked up, his eyes meeting hers, and the amusement in them showed he knew she'd been watching him. 'But we're on our honeymoon,' he protested.

Tasha gritted her teeth.

'Chaz,' she said.

'Yes Tasha,' said Chaz.

'Do you have any contraceptives now?'

He looked at her warily.

'Yes,' he said. 'I got some a couple of days ago.'

Just as she'd thought. As far as he was concerned, the result was a foregone conclusion.

'Even after what we agreed?'

'I thought we agreed I could do what I usually do,' he said drily. 'You told me that the day we got here.'

'But—'

'Just because I'm not out looking doesn't mean something couldn't turn up. You can't predict these things, so it's better to be prepared.'

'So you're not hoping I'll change my mind,' she said accusingly.

'Of course I'm hoping you'll change your mind.' A black eyebrow shot up in extravagant mockery. 'I was half hoping the sight of me in a wet towel might tip the balance, but it doesn't seem to have worked. Maybe I should do a few more sit-ups.'

'You look fine,' said Tasha.

'I was hoping for irresistible,' said Chaz.

'Sorry to disappoint you,' Tasha said loftily.

He grinned. 'Liar. You'd like to look me up and down and tell me it doesn't do a thing for you.'

'What is this radio station, anyway?' asked Tasha desperately.

'Somebody else's problem,' said Chaz. 'Ever made love to a man in a wet towel?'

'No,' said Tasha.

'You don't know what you're missing. I don't mean me personally, obviously, just the towel factor.' There was a glint in his eyes. 'Lie down beside me for a moment and let me demonstrate.'

'*No,*' said Tasha.

Chaz raised an eyebrow. 'C'mon, Tash, even if you don't like it how much worse can it be than five thousand paintings in five days? I'm not breaking our agreement, mind, just arranging a scientific demonstration.' He put a hand on her shoulder and pulled her down beside him.

She knew she should just sit up again. It would have been easy enough to do—his hand was still on her shoulder, but he wasn't putting much muscle behind it. It was the smile in his eyes that held her.

'That's right,' he said. 'Now straighten your legs...' His eyes, inches away from hers, were brilliant with amusement. 'Good. Just a little closer...' She was so close she could smell the faint fragrance of the hotel's soap, and underlying it the masculine scent of his skin.

'Now,' said Chaz, 'if I hook my free leg over yours, like this...'

One long, damp leg, bare to the hip where the towel had fallen free, lay the length of hers.

'Fine,' said Tasha. 'You've made your point—'

'And if you put your hand on my waist,' he said, placing her hand at the edge of the towel, 'anything could happen. It's the element of suspense, you see.' His eyes held hers. 'One of us might make a careless movement. You might pull the towel off by accident; we might be so close to each other we didn't notice at first.' He was so close she could feel his breath on her mouth. 'Or,' he said softly, 'I might feel your hand on the knot, and realise you were untying

it on purpose.' A smile quirked at the corner of his mouth.
'Can you feel the tension?'

She could feel the blood pounding in her veins.

'No,' she said huskily.

'Well,' he said, 'maybe you should move your hand. Put
it on my leg.'

His bare leg lay on top of hers, slightly curved. She put
her hand on it near the knee.

'No, higher up,' he said.

She slid her hand up the powerful muscle of his thigh.
His eyes closed for a moment, and she left her hand splayed
on the sleek bare skin.

'The thing is,' he said softly, his eyes still closed, 'now
I don't know what you'll do next. You might move your
hand up just a little...you might move it up under the
towel...'

He opened his eyes.

'You see what I mean,' he said, eyes gleaming. 'And
you can do that with any man in a towel.'

'I don't *want* to do it with any man in a towel,' said
Tasha.

'Well, that's obviously a decision only you can make,'
said Chaz. 'But naturally I'm pleased.'

Tasha began to shake with laughter.

'Careful,' said Chaz. 'Towel alert.'

Tasha laughed out loud. 'You're impossible,' she said.

'I know,' said Chaz. His eyes met hers, still with that
lurking smile. 'Kiss me,' he said.

Her eyes held his. 'Why?' she said. 'So I'll know what
it's like to kiss a man in a wet towel?'

He shook his head. 'No,' he said. 'Just because I'd like
you to.'

Tasha felt a moment's despair. Practically a whole week
and five thousand artistic masterpieces down the drain. But
maybe she could start again tomorrow. Museums with

paintings 'attributed to the school of so and so'. Churches with 'poorly restored font, fresco destroyed by damp though lower right-hand corner partially visible'. Cemeteries with the nephew of a cousin of Balzac.

She bent her head forward and brushed her mouth across his.

She could hear his sudden sharp intake of breath, feel the sudden stir of his loins where he was pressed against her.

She drew her head back, propping it on her hand.

'Give up, Tasha,' said Chaz. 'It's never going to work.'

'What?'

'You could take me to see every item in every museum in the country and then start over again; you could go through Paris brick by brick with a guidebook and I'd still want you.' She could feel desire uncurling inside her at the unashamed hunger in his eyes.

'Until you'd had me, anyway,' she said coolly.

An eyebrow flicked up. 'Well, there's only one way to find out,' he said. He gave her a rather mocking smile. 'Which you're not inclined to try.' He slid his leg off hers and sat up, adjusting the towel.

Tasha sat up beside him, watching him warily.

'You don't have to do anything you don't want to do,' he said. 'As I keep saying. Just promise me you'll do something you actually want to do for a change.'

'There's nothing I particularly—' This was too much like a confession of guilt, and she stopped abruptly.

'Then let me think of something I think you'd like.' He gave her a lurking smile. 'Apart from the obvious. Will you leave everything to me?'

She nodded. What else could she do? She could hardly suggest Gloves of France through the Ages now.

'Good. Then I'll be off for another refreshing shower.'

'*Oh,*' said Tasha. She gave him a rather quizzical smile.

# MILLS & BOON®

## An Important Message from The Editors of Mills & Boon®

Dear Reader,

Because you've chosen to read one of our romance novels, we'd like to say "thank you"!

And, as a **special way** to thank you, we've selected <u>four more</u> of the <u>books</u> you love so much **and** a welcome gift to send you absolutely <u>FREE!</u>

Please enjoy them with our compliments...

*Tessa Shapcott*

Editor, Mills & Boon

P.S. And because we value our customers we've attached something extra inside...

PEEL OFF AND PLACE INSIDE

# How to validate your Editor's Free Gift "Thank You"

1. **Peel off the Free Gift Seal** from the front cover. Place it in the space provided to the right. This automatically entitles you to receive four free books and a beautiful goldtone book locket.

2. **Complete your details** on the card, detach along the dotted line, and post it back to us. No stamp needed. We'll then send you four selected romances from the Enchanted™ series. These books have a retail value of at least £2.20, but are yours to keep absolutely free.

3. **Enjoy the read.** We hope that after receiving your free books you'll want to remain a subscriber. But the choice is yours - to continue or cancel, any time at all! So why not accept our no risk invitation? You'll be glad you did.

**Your satisfaction is guaranteed**
You're under no obligation to buy anything. We charge you nothing for your introductory parcel. And you don't have to make any minimum number of purchases – not even one! Thousands of readers have already discovered that the Reader Service is the most convenient way of enjoying the latest new romance novels before they are available in the shops. Of course, postage and packing is completely FREE.

*Tessa Shapcott*
Editor, Mills & Boon

# Yours FREE...
## when you reply today

This delicate book locket is a necklace with a difference... The hinged book is decorated with a romantic floral motive and opens to reveal two oval frames for your most cherished photographs. Respond today and it's yours free.

# Yes! Please send me my four FREE books and a welcome gift

FREE GIFT SEAL

**Yes!** I have placed my free gift seal in the space provided above. Please send me my four free books along with my welcome gift. I understand I am under no obligation to purchase any books, as explained on the back and opposite page. I am over 18 years of age.

N9HI

Surname (Mrs/Ms/Miss/Mr) _____Initials_____

Address _____

_____

_____

_____Postcode _____

▶ Detach and keep your complimentary book mark. ▶

**HOW THE READER SERVICE WORKS**

Accepting the free books places you under no obligation to buy anything. You may keep the books and gift and return the despatch note marked "cancel". If we don't hear from you, about a month later we will send you 6 brand new books and invoice you for only £2.40* each. That's the complete price – there is no extra charge for postage and packing. You may cancel at any time, otherwise every month we'll send you 6 more books, which you may either purchase or return – the choice is yours.

*Terms and prices subject to change without notice.

The Reader Service™
FREEPOST CN81
CROYDON
CR9 3WZ

NO
STAMP
NEEDED

'Well,' she said, 'in that case I'd better kiss you properly, hadn't I?'

She turned so that she sat facing him, half kneeling, with her legs out to one side. She put one hand in his slick wet hair, pulling his head down to her, and pressed her mouth to his in a long, sensuous kiss that was calculated to send the blood pressure rocketing. All her plans lay in ruins, and there was just one hope left. Maybe he'd catch pneumonia in the shower.

# CHAPTER SIX

THEIR second week in Paris was very different from the first. They spent a lot of time walking through the streets, exploring the various quarters on foot. Sometimes they would come by accident on a street market and wander along, looking at the stalls and arguing over what and whether to buy. They would walk along the river, browsing in the secondhand book stalls, pretending to look for rare editions of Spinoza for the professor. At night they went to a club where Chaz's friends were playing, and then to other clubs, and came home late. In the morning they would get up for a late breakfast, and sometimes sit talking at the café for a couple of hours.

Tasha had to admit she was having a good time. She wondered whether she hadn't overreacted at first. Maybe she had felt herself to be more vulnerable and susceptible than she really was, and worried accordingly. The shift from the frenzy of the pre-wedding period to having it all behind her had been very sudden, and it had been a shock to find herself suddenly alone with Chaz. Now she was beginning to relax—or maybe it was that she felt she was beginning to understand him better.

They had really had rather similar backgrounds, she thought, except that his had been twenty times more shifting and uncertain than hers. The cast of characters in his life had changed every year or so—she thought it was one of the reasons her father had made a point of staying in touch.

They had each had to find their own way of coping. Hers had been to try to please everybody. His had been to please no one but himself. She had tried to make every relationship permanent, no matter what the cost. He had had relationships no longer than the amusement they offered him. He had infuriated her, of course, but at least he had made something of his life, which was more than she could say.

On the last day before they were to leave they had another of their long, leisurely breakfasts. Tasha was wearing a sleeveless dark blue Nehru top and brown jodhpur trousers with brown ankle boots; she had managed to combine casual with chic in a way that made her comfortable around Chaz without making her too conscious of having dressed to impress.

'Will you kill me if I mention the word "museum"?' he asked. 'There's something you really ought to see.'

Tasha reddened, thinking of the way she had singlemindedly dedicated her first week there to seeing that he had as horrible a time as possible. Chaz had spent the last seven days singlemindedly making sure she had a marvellous time—the contrast was embarrassing. 'What is it?' she asked.

'There are two rooms of water lilies by Monet at the Orangerie. It's pretty amazing—they take up whole walls. You can't really get an idea from a book.'

They went to the museum and it was just as he had said.

The water lilies took up two enormous rooms in the basement of the museum. Across the immense stretches of canvas the water glimmered and glittered or retreated into misty shadows, the lilies floating on its surface, in great symphonies of colour that changed with the time of day. Tasha walked up and down drinking in the colour-drenched walls.

'They're marvellous,' she said, pulling out a stupid little word because no word could say what she felt.

'Yes,' he said simply.

He added, after a pause, 'He actually created these water

gardens down by the river, you know. You can still see them. They've been restored.'

'You mean this is a real place?' she said incredulously.

He smiled at her disbelief. 'Tell you what, why don't we drive over today? I'll rent a car.'

Tasha was still trying to get used to Chaz's way of doing things. If he decided to do something he jumped in feet first. The idea of marrying someone on the spur of the moment had been absolutely in character.

Within the hour he had rented a car and was driving her up to Normandy to Monet's gardens at Giverny.

The gardens near the house were brilliant with daffodils and tulips and irises. They walked through the spring flowers down to the water, and there was the famous Japanese bridge, there were the willow trees, there were the great lily pads floating here on black water, there on bright patches of sky.

'It's hard to believe it's part of the real world,' said Tasha. 'That we're actually *walking* here.'

'I know what you mean,' he said. He smiled. 'It reminds me of you, funnily enough.'

'Sorry?'

'You never quite seem to belong to the real world somehow,' he said. 'Hard to believe sometimes that you're flesh and blood like the rest of us.'

Tasha gave him a startled look.

He took her hand in his and looked down at it. 'But here you are, with a ring on your finger and clothes from a shop in Chelsea.'

She did not want to snatch her hand away, not after the last week, but she wished it didn't feel like a needle suddenly stuck to a magnet. She smiled vaguely and replied almost at random, 'It's so quiet here. So lovely and peaceful.' Soon she would be in New York, trying to live at the pace of the fastest city in the world. A faint sense of unease crossed her mind. She thought she was getting on all right with Chaz now, but what would it be like in a place as fast and impatient as he was?

She turned to run her fingers over a strand of willow leaves, so that her hand left his naturally. A duck flew quacking across the water and landed with a splash. The path had brought them back again to the Japanese bridge, and she walked onto it to lean on the rail and look down. He came to her side and leant on the rail beside her, looking down to the water where their two faces were mirrored in the shimmering water.

'How do you feel now?' he asked her. 'I know it hasn't been very long. Still feeling pretty bruised about Jeremy?'

Tasha realised suddenly that she hadn't thought about Jeremy in days. The last time she *had* thought of him it had been to think how nice it was that he wasn't there.

'I, er,' she said. She felt an overwhelming temptation to say something noncommittal, implying without saying in so many words that she was gradually, with great difficulty, getting over this traumatic event. But it wasn't fair, not when Chaz had tried so hard.

'I know it's awful,' she said. 'But I haven't thought of him in days. Whenever I think of him I'm just glad he isn't here.' She was looking at her reflection in the water, not at Chaz. That glimmering girl yards below had thought she was in love with someone. Now she was standing beside someone very handsome, not looking at him. 'I'm sorry about the first week,' she was saying. 'I just overreacted. It was hard to trust anybody. I just wanted to keep everyone at a safe distance.'

'I know,' he said.

'I've had a wonderful time,' she was saying.

'So have I,' he said.

The man in the water was looking at the girl. He probably wanted to kiss her. Was that so terrible?

'Natasha,' said Chaz. The man was leaning closer. 'Natasha,' said Chaz. 'This is probably too soon, but…' The man was looking at the girl and hesitating. 'There's something I wanted to say to you.' He was probably thinking that he had promised not to, but that it was a stupid promise.

Tasha turned her head. His face was just inches from hers. 'It's all right,' she said. She raised her mouth to his and kissed him. He was probably thinking that it was stupid to deny yourself a physical pleasure when it was so delicious. He was probably thinking the reason this kiss was better than all the others, the reason every kiss had been better than the ones before, was that the here and now is always better than a memory. He put his hand on her head, his fingers tangling in her hair.

They spent the day at the gardens, watching the light change in the sky and on the water, talking or not talking as the mood took them. They went back to Paris in the early evening. Chaz seemed restless and edgy—well, that quiet day probably wasn't the kind of thing he would normally have chosen. He shifted from subject to subject, telling a series of brilliant anecdotes with a kind of rapid, hard wit that entertained without engaging. Tasha just hoped he hadn't been too bored.

They returned the car, and then had dinner at a small restaurant which Chaz said he'd always liked when he'd lived in Paris before. Afterwards Tasha said she still hadn't had enough of walking—in London people only went out on the streets to go from A to B, whereas in Paris you always felt what was going on between A and B was probably more interesting than either.

They walked into the great forecourt of the Louvre, where the glass pyramid laid its floating reflection in the surrounding pool. Someone was playing a flute somewhere, and tourists sat along the banks of the pool talking softly.

They lingered awhile, exchanging jokes about the artistic treasures they'd seen, then walked on towards the river, crossing a pedestrian bridge. Three buskers were playing jazz halfway across the bridge; Tasha's steps slowed.

On impulse she said, 'Do you mind if we stop? We're not really going anywhere.'

'Sure,' said Chaz. He dropped some money in the hat. They sat down on a bench, not talking. It was a warm, soft night; a full moon was rising. It would obviously have been more romantic, Tasha thought, if she'd been here with someone she was madly in love with—but it was fun anyway just being in Paris, doing things on the spur of the moment. She couldn't really imagine Jeremy just stopping on a bridge to listen to people who were playing for spare change.

Other people came and sat down, or got up and left. Some of the people listening seemed to be friends of the buskers—once or twice someone would swap places with one of the original musicians. Then someone came up to Chaz. A rapid conversation in French broke out, which, as far as Tasha could follow, went:

'Hey, it's you!'

'Hey, it's you!'

'What are you doing here?'

'I'm on my honeymoon. This is my wife.'

Tasha couldn't really understand the reply to this, which involved vocabulary not usually made available to students preparing for GCSE. There was a pause. 'Does she speak French?'

'Some. What are you doing here?' said Chaz.

'What do you think? Look, why don't you play something?'

'Are you crazy? Do you know how long it's been?'

More off-syllabus vocabulary seemed to be aimed at the venue and audience. The gist seemed to be that it didn't matter how long it had been because they were on a bridge playing for tourists who wouldn't know the difference.

Chaz finally shrugged and grinned and took over from the bass player for a couple of pieces. In Tasha's opinion as an uninformed tourist it sounded a lot better than the man who'd been playing before.

A lot of other uninformed tourists seemed to think so too—a shower of coins and a couple of banknotes fell into the hat. The previous player made a few more pungent comments, then broke off suddenly, his eye caught by someone coming across the bridge.

Tasha looked too. A girl was coming towards them. She had very short, bleached hair, and huge, kohl-rimmed eyes, and very pale beestung lips. She was wearing a leather mini and a fake leopardskin top and thigh-length black boots with big platform soles. As she came closer she caught sight of Chaz and shrieked, 'Chaz! *C'est toi!*'

She broke into a run, shouting a lot of things that left Tasha floundering back at 'Chaz! It's you!' The three buskers wound down the piece, while the newcomer flung her arms around Chaz's and kissed him enthusiastically on his cheeks, mouth and anything else in reach.

Chaz was grinning. There was another conversation Tasha couldn't follow. Then he said in English, 'But there's someone I'd like you to meet. Toni, this is my wife, Natasha. Tasha, Toni's an old friend of mine.'

The huge eyes widened further. 'You are—married?'

There was no mistaking that look of terrible disappointment.

'On my honeymoon,' said Chaz. 'We ran into Jean-Luc by coincidence and he insisted I stand in for him. Speaking of which, I'd better get back to work.'

'Then I go with you,' said Toni. 'I sing, yes? It will be just like old times.'

They went back to the other buskers and Toni launched

into 'The Man Who Got Away'. There was no mistaking
the man she had in mind, either. There was a bittersweet
curve to her mouth each time she glanced at Chaz. Tasha
felt a little prickle of—what? Not jealousy, surely—just a
sudden sense of exclusion. Because it was obvious the two
had done this together so many times before. And because
it was obvious that the girl was spectacularly good. She
had a lovely, smoky voice; the combination of this with
the French accent just brushing over the words was at once
poignant and seductive. Money rained into the hat. Chaz
was looking down at the girl beside him.

Tasha dropped her eyes. Then suddenly the moment was
gone. Next thing Tasha knew Chaz had swept them all,
wife, buskers, understudies and a few discerning members
of the audience, off to a bar where they all sat around
laughing and talking at the top of their voices and drinking
champagne.

Under cover of the noise Tasha could not help asking
Toni, 'You know Chaz well?'

The French girl answered the question she hadn't asked.
'We were not lovers,' she said, with another of those bittersweet smiles. 'I was just a baby when we met, you
know? I ran away from home, I was sleeping on the streets,
he helped me out. That's all.'

Tasha stared at her. All this time she'd been imagining
Chaz's one true love as someone very sweet and conven-
tional. Never in her wildest dreams could she have come
up with someone like this. But wasn't Toni much more
*likely* a girl for Chaz to fall in love with? 'I didn't want to
rush her,' he'd said. Who knew how young Toni had been
when they'd met? And if she'd been vulnerable he wouldn't
have wanted to take advantage of that. Chaz had seen
something in this brave, talented, streetwise girl, and then
something had happened…

She glanced at Chaz, who was roaring with laughter at

some unrepeatable joke. He didn't *look* heartbroken. It was only too obvious, though, that Toni had regrets for what might have been. Tasha felt guilty for letting her think Chaz was definitely out of reach. But then Chaz had brought up the marriage at the first possible opportunity. Was that his way of telling the girl that what was past was past?

Jean-Luc said something to Toni, who shrugged and nodded. 'OK, OK,' she said. 'Chaz, it was great to see you again. Tasha, it was nice to meet you.'

'Call me if you come to New York,' said Chaz.

'Yeah, sure,' said Toni. She stood up, sketched a wave with one hand, and walked off, Jean-Luc's arm around her shoulders.

Then everyone walked off through the dark streets, the crowd gradually breaking up as people went their separate ways, and then Tasha and Chaz were alone together again.

'It's a wonderful city, isn't it?' she said. 'Things just happen. People just turn up and have a wonderful time. It's magical.'

He laughed. 'Well, there may be just as many people who live for the moment in London, but by and large they don't do it in public. That may have something to do with it.'

'Yes,' said Tasha. 'Toni was amazing,' she said. 'She's got a wonderful voice.'

'Yes, she's very talented,' said Chaz. 'She's improved a lot since the last time I saw her—she should do well.' He didn't sound consumed with regrets. Had she just imagined everything?

'I've never had such a good time in my life,' she said. She'd thrown it out as an expression of polite enthusiasm, but it occurred to her, suddenly, that it was actually true. She'd never had such a wonderful day in all her life. She didn't want it to end. 'What do we do now?'

He gave a crack of laughter. 'Now we go back to the hotel,' he said.

'Oh,' said Tasha.

'But first,' said Chaz, 'we stop walking.' He came to a halt, and Tasha stopped beside him. He looked down at her, his eyes brilliant in the dark shadow of his brow. 'And now I kiss you,' he said. 'Not just because I've been thinking of nothing else for the past week, but also because we're in Paris and there's a full moon and it would be a crime not to.'

He bent his head and kissed her. Tasha had been drinking champagne for the last three hours; maybe that was why her head swam as soon as his mouth touched hers. His words had been rather flippant, but his mouth was hot and hungry. He devoured her as if he had been thinking of nothing else for months rather than days. She'd been wondering rather irritably why this morning didn't count, but it was only too obvious why it didn't count. She clung to him, melting against him.

The walk back to the hotel was magical. Moonlight bathed the streets. Every so often they would pass a strange, unwanted-looking streetlight with a dull yellow or orange glow. The rest of the time they walked from silver to black to silver again.

They picked up the keys at Reception, then went upstairs. Every night for the last two weeks he had kissed her on the cheek outside her door. Every night she'd gone into her room and he'd gone into his room alone.

They stood by her door.

'Goodnight, Tasha,' said Chaz, and he kissed her on the cheek.

He was waiting for her to go in. She turned the key in the door and opened it, and he turned away and walked on to his own room.

Tasha stepped reluctantly into her room. The look on

Toni's face came back to her—that look of someone who had had a chance that would not come again. Did she want to look that way? Did she want to wonder all her life?

Her room was dark, with broad silver bands of moonlight streaming in through the windows and across the bed and carpet. Outside it was still that magical moonlit night. Suddenly, without giving herself time to think, she closed her door without walking through it, and turned the key.

She walked up behind him just as he was walking into his room, and followed him in.

'Chaz?' she said.

'Natasha?'

The bands of silver moonlight streamed in from these windows too.

'Does it have to be goodnight?' she said.

He closed the door behind her.

'You know it doesn't have to be,' he said. He raised a hand to her hair and smoothed back the bright strands.

'For instance,' he said softly, 'I could kiss you again.'

His mouth found hers, and again she found her head spinning, as if all the champagne she had drunk had suddenly foamed up inside her.

He raised his head. His black eyes glittered in the dark. 'Or,' he said even more softly, 'I could undress you.'

She had half expected an argument, more last minute scruples, at least an Are you sure? But his hand was already at the neck of her blouse, slipping the first button through its hole. His mouth brushed hers again.

'Would you like that?' he asked, his breath warm on her cheek, but he didn't wait for an answer. His fingers were at the second button. She turned her head so that her mouth met his again, and she slipped her tongue into his mouth. The third button had already come free; she could feel her breath come more quickly. His thumb pushed the fourth and fifth buttons through.

The stubble on his cheek pricked her skin as he moved his mouth away. 'I could put my hand on your breast,' he said, his voice grazing her ear. 'Would you like that?' She shivered as his warm hand slid over her skin. 'Oh, God, you're not wearing a bra, how lovely.' The soft laugh in his voice caressed her as his thumb dragged over her nipple. He kissed her again.

She turned her head again so that her cheek was against his. 'Or I could undress you,' she said. 'Would you like that?'

'Yes,' he said. There was the ghost of laughter in his voice. 'I'd like that very much.'

He was wearing a jacket, a T-shirt and dark canvas trousers. She slipped the jacket back over his shoulders so that it fell to the ground. She slid her hands under the T-shirt and began rolling it up his chest until it was bunched up under his arms. 'Bend your head,' she said, and he bent his head so that she could pull it forward over his head and down over the powerful shoulders and arms.

She dropped the T-shirt to the floor and began to unbuckle his belt.

She thought suddenly of the way he had lingered over every button.

'I'm sorry, I'm going too fast,' she said, looking up to meet his eyes.

'Isn't that supposed to be my line?' he said smiling. 'You couldn't possibly.'

Tasha could feel her cheeks go hot. She finished unbuckling the belt with hurrying, clumsy fingers, unzipped the stiff zip and pushed his trousers down over his hips. They fell to his feet; he had to slip out of his shoes because she hadn't thought of that in time, and then he stepped out of his trousers and he still probably thought she was taking too long.

'I didn't mean that the way you—I just meant that you're

lovely,' he said. 'I'd better not say anything else in case I say the wrong thing.' He pulled her into his arms again and kissed her lingeringly, his mouth exploring hers until her knees were weak. His hand found the side zip of her jodhpurs. It was stiff too, and she could feel his fingers tugging at the little tongue of metal, and somehow that moment of awkwardness brought home to her his experience in a way that even his earlier practised ease had not. He felt none of the embarrassment she would have felt; instead he had somehow managed to give the momentary difficulty an erotic charge of its own. His hand lay along the curve of her hip; his thumb and forefinger eased the blade of metal down, using its slow, uneven progress against the resisting metal track to heighten her awareness. Then the zip slid suddenly easily down, and his mouth was still ravishing hers with kisses. It was lovely, of course it was lovely, that was why she was here, but she felt completely out of her depth.

Her boots and jodhpurs were removed with that same unnervingly unhurried control.

'Mmm,' said Chaz. 'And what shall we do now?'

'Isn't that fairly obvious?' she said edgily.

He ran a thumb across her mouth, then put his mouth where his thumb had been. 'It's your wedding night,' he said softly. 'Your real wedding night. I want it to be something special.'

Nerves were pushing her to break the mood, to make a joke, to be matter-of-fact. 'I'm sure it will be fine,' she said.

He laughed. 'As good as that.'

He stroked her hair back with one hand. 'Well, you don't need this,' he said, sliding her top back down her arms and dropping it. 'Or these,' he added, placing his hands on her hips and sliding her last scrap of protection down her legs to the floor.

Tasha looked down at him. He was squatting at her feet, looking up and smiling at her. 'Ever made love according to a Japanese haiku poem?' he asked.

'What?' she asked blankly.

'Pale petals on white snow,' he said. 'The rose unfurls. A storm shakes the flower.'

She shook her head. She realised ruefully that she was thinking mainly that it was her turn to finish undressing him.

'You don't know what you're missing,' he said.

'Oh,' she said, still striving for a light note. 'Is it like making love to a man in a wet towel, then?'

'No, nothing like that,' he said. He stood up. 'Come on over to the bed.' He scooped her up into his arms and strode over to the enormous bed.

'Do you remember telling me I was selfish for suggesting you spend the night with me?' he asked, still not putting her down.

'Yes, well, obviously I—'

Chaz grinned at her. 'Didn't know what you were missing,' he said. 'I should take you through this poem five times and make you apologise.' He set her down on the bed and sat down beside her. 'Assuming my self-control held out that long.'

'What are you—?'

'Pale petals on white snow,' he said. He bent his head and kissed her breast, his tongue teasing her nipple. She drew in a sharp breath. 'Somebody must have wanted to tell someone,' he said softly, 'that her breasts were as white as snow in the moonlight.' A breath of laughter warmed his voice. 'Only he couldn't come right out and say it.' His mouth moved to her other breast. She closed her eyes.

His hand moved down the line of her hip to her thigh. He raised his head. His dark eyes held hers as his hand moved between her thighs. 'The rose unfurls petal by petal,' he said softly. He kissed her mouth. 'You're so beautiful,' he said. 'Your eyes are so wild. I always wondered what they would look like...'

His touch was as light as if he had really been coaxing a rose to unfurl, as light as his breath on her cheek, the murmur of his voice in her ear. She felt as though she was drowning in sweetness, and still his eyes held hers; it was as if words were too clumsy for the things she might want, as if his eyes had to ask Do you like this? and read the answer in her face.

The intent, listening look on his face reminded her of something, and suddenly it came to her. In her mind she saw him on a bridge, laughing and saying, 'Do you know how long it's been?' and then shrugging and taking the instrument thrust in his hands. It had been just a battered old thing, nothing special, and in the hands of its owner it had sounded like the ordinary thing it was. In her mind she saw Chaz standing with the other musicians, saw his long, clever fingers on the strings, saw his face *listening*, not just to the sound but to the instrument he was bringing to life.

His fingers were moving harder and faster. His eyes were still looking into her face. He was listening to her body the way he had listened to the instrument, but it was not his fault that she was thinking it; his eyes said that she was lovely, she was like a flower shaken by a storm. He bent his head to kiss her again.

Even as she shuddered with pleasure she was already thinking, in some back corner of her mind, that she must not take too long, that it was her turn to do something for him, that he was waiting for her to finish—all the things she had always remembered even when the man was in love with her, and if it was important to remember then how much more important to remember with someone who wasn't in love. If she did something perhaps it would blot out the unwanted images that had come to her.

She tried to sit up, remembering that she should finish undressing him. He pushed her back down to the bed. His face had an odd expression, a strange mixture of amusement and implacability.

'Natasha,' he said, his voice caressing the syllables. 'Don't be in such a hurry.' His mouth brushed hers. 'Ever had five desserts before dinner?'

'No.' She could hardly breathe.

'You don't know what you're missing.'

She felt as if she was melting under the sweetness of his touch. Gradually the uncomfortable images softened and blurred, drowned out by sheer physical sensation. She lost track of time, but she thought it must have been a long time later when she realised she was looking into his eyes without thinking that she must do something. She felt only that she wanted him.

She raised her hands to his waist and peeled his briefs down without embarrassment, his nakedness now as natural to her as her own. He took a packet of contraceptives from the bedside table, opened one and put it on.

He knelt between her legs, looking down into her face for a moment. Then he leant forward, his hands just above her shoulders, and then he was inside her.

He lowered himself onto his forearms. His eyes held hers in shared awareness of the movement inside her from even this slight shifting of his weight. 'Natasha,' he said. 'God, you're lovely. You're so lovely.' He kissed her hard.

Chaz lay back on the bed, an arm stretched out on the pillow, the moonlight falling in white slashes across him. His eyes were dark and brilliant in the shadow of his brows, the planes of his face sharply defined in the silver light.

Tasha lay on her side, head propped on an elbow, watching him. She didn't really know what to think. It seemed stupid, but somehow she'd never thought of sex as something like other physical activities, something involving a range of skills. Things a musician would do better than other people. Things an athlete would do better than other people.

Well, now she knew her mistake. Chaz outclassed everyone she'd ever been involved with the way a Wimbledon first seed outclasses the amateur who volleys a few balls with a friend on weekends. He outclassed them the way a virtuoso outclasses someone who's still struggling with the scales. And she hadn't even known there were classes. She hadn't realised it was a competition.

She had probably tried more positions in the past few hours than she had in the whole eight years since she'd slept with her first boyfriend. 'Tell me what you like,' Chaz had said. 'Do you like this? Or this?' Again and again he had used his taut, hard body, with its strength and its stamina, to push her to peaks of pleasure she hadn't known existed. He had once talked of fireworks—it really had felt as if he'd been setting off explosions inside her.

She hadn't known it could be like that, and of course it had been wonderful. But somehow it had felt odd. She'd been in love the other times, or had thought she was, and it had been part of being in love, whereas now it was just—well, what? Not empty, exactly, but not all that different from earlier on when they'd drunk champagne. She'd had a marvellous time then too, but then she'd never thought of drinking champagne as the ultimate expression of your love for someone.

She sighed. He was so *beautiful*, beautiful and dangerous—nobody had any right to look that beautiful. Why couldn't she just enjoy it for what it was, the way he did?

'You all right, Tash?' he asked softly.

'Of course,' said Tasha. 'It was wonderful.'

'But?'

'No, it was wonderful,' said Tasha. 'It's just—' She broke off.

'It's just what?' he said, a smile in his voice. 'Something you'd like me to do? Don't be shy, darling, I'm completely unshockable.'

Tasha shook her head. 'Nothing like that,' she said. 'It's just that I've never slept with someone I wasn't in love with before. It was wonderful, but it just felt rather—odd.'

'Oh, I see. I'm sorry.'

'No, it was wonderful—'

'You don't have to keep saying it was wonderful,' Chaz said edgily.

'It's just that it meant something different the other times,' she said. 'So it was almost as if I were lying. I know it doesn't feel that way to you.'

'No,' he said. 'It didn't feel that way to me.' He reached up a hand to stroke her hair. 'Poor Tash,' he said. 'I know it must all seem a bit sudden. I suppose I shouldn't have rushed you into it—it just felt right somehow, and I tend to go with my instincts on these things.'

'I shouldn't have said anything,' Tasha said remorsefully. 'It's not that I didn't enjoy it. It was much better than it's ever been before. And you didn't rush me into it—' Something pricked her memory, then was gone. 'I wanted to. I just felt a bit odd afterwards. It was such a physical thing.'

'Well, what else would it be?' he said rather wearily.

'I don't know,' she said.

He stroked her hair for a moment in silence. 'Well, never mind,' he said at last. 'We don't have to do it again, Tash— I'm not taking anything for granted. Just put it down to Paris. Too much champagne, too much moonlight; it all went to your head and you had a fling. You won't be a different person when you wake up in the morning.'

'I know,' she said. She sighed. 'I know I shouldn't have

said anything,' she said. 'It's just—when we were making love I felt as if I were a part of you. It felt odd to have thoughts in my head that I was keeping from you, and when you asked what I was thinking it felt natural to tell you. But now I feel as if I've spoiled it for you.'

He laughed softly. 'You couldn't do that, Tash.' He ran a finger along the line of her jaw before allowing his hand to drop to his side. 'A magical day and a magical night. Who could ask for more?'

Tasha stared at him. Knowing Chaz, she couldn't believe he could say something like that and actually mean it. There had to be a note of irony that she'd missed. But he was still watching her with those dark, brilliant eyes; as far as she could tell there wasn't a trace of mockery in his face.

'Thank you,' she said uncertainly.

'My pleasure,' said Chaz. Well, there was no mistaking the note of mockery there, anyway. He sat up and stretched, flexing the powerful arm muscles, then yawned suddenly. 'Magical but—taxing,' he said grinning. 'We'd better get some sleep, Tash. Want me to clear out so you can have the bed to yourself?'

'This is your bed,' Tasha pointed out.

'I don't mind. Want me to go next door? That way you can wake up alone.'

'N-no,' said Tasha. 'You don't have to do that. Not unless you want to.'

'I'm not the one who felt odd,' he said. 'Don't feel you have to be polite.'

'I'm not being polite,' she said. 'I'd rather you stayed.'

'Then the ayes have it.'

He lay down again beside her. It felt odd not to be touching him, so she slid over until she lay next to him, and he put an arm around her and went to sleep.

Tasha woke to brilliant sunlight. In place of the magical room of light and dark was a beautiful but distinctly unmagical hotel room. She was lying in a rumpled, distinctly unmagical bed. She was lying in the arms of a naked, distinctly unmagical—

Oh, *no*.

She turned her head cautiously. She was lying in the arms of a man who needed a shave. Not a fairytale prince, just her handsome, selfish, cynical sort-of cousin, who'd no doubt been through this more times than he could count. Japanese *poems*? From *Chaz*? They must have slipped something in the champagne to make her fall for that. Well, she'd had the come-on and now she'd have the brush-off. Maybe she should just go and have a shower.

She tried to extricate herself from his arms. They tightened round her. His eyes opened. She'd been steeling herself for whatever look Chaz did give women when he was ready to move on, but his face lit up with a smile.

'My God, so I didn't dream it,' he said. 'It really happened.'

Tasha gave him the sort of smile that says 'er' as clearly as any words.

He laughed. 'Don't you just hate it when your prince turns into a frog?'

'I wouldn't say that—' began Tasha.

'But it's never going to happen again. I remember.' He gave her a look sparkling with amusement. 'Of course, we never did thrash out the details of exactly *what* wasn't going to happen again.'

In spite of herself she could feel her own mouth curving up.

'Mind if I kiss you?' He was tracing one of her flyaway eyebrows with his thumb. 'I'd like you to kiss me just once in broad daylight, when you can see what you're doing.'

'I kissed you in broad daylight yesterday,' said Tasha.

'Yes,' said Chaz. 'But that was when I had all my clothes on.'

Tasha began to laugh helplessly. For some reason which she did not understand, the cold, empty feeling of the night before, when he had been so dangerous and beautiful, had melted away. In place of the romantic stranger she had her abominable, unshaven and, as he had pointed out, completely naked non-cousin pelting her with jokes, and laughter kept bubbling up inside her. 'Oh, Chaz, you're impossible,' she said.

'I know,' he said, smiling down at her. 'But what do you expect? I'm in a state of shock. I can't believe you did it. Bet you can't believe you did it, either.'

Tasha was still laughing. 'Oh, Chaz,' she said again. She put her hand up to his rough cheek.

He bent his head and kissed her. His mouth was soft and warm, ravishing in its sweetness; it was as if she'd forgotten in just a few hours what it was like, and yet it was as if she'd never known what it was like because she'd never kissed him with that sudden, surprising mixture of laughter and liking. It was as if the coldness the night before had been an effect of the moonlight, and now the sun was up.

A long time later he raised his head. He was still smiling at her. 'Tasha,' he said.

'Yes, Chaz,' she said, smiling back.

'There's something I have to tell you. I should have told you before, but…'

'But what?'

'But…' He brushed her mouth with his. 'I got distracted…'

The telephone rang on the bedside table. He kissed her again.

'You know,' said Chaz, 'I think we should stay here another couple of weeks. We could just stay in bed all day

not doing all the things we're never going to do again.
What do you think?'

'The telephone's ringing,' said Tasha.

'We could take showers together and not do anything in
the shower,' said Chaz. 'Then we could go back to not
doing anything in bed. Make up for all the time we wasted
in separate bedrooms.'

'The phone—' said Tasha.

'God, you're beautiful,' he said. 'You're so fantastically
beautiful.'

'What was it you wanted to tell me?' asked Tasha.

Chaz reached over impatiently, picked up the receiver
and slammed it down.

There was a moment of silence. He turned back to her
in the rumpled bed.

He said, 'I was thinking about what you said last night.'

There was something faintly eerie about the silent phone.

Chaz said, 'You sounded so—desolate. I was thinking it
was probably my fault for—'

The phone began to ring again.

'Chaz, do you think we should—?'

'I don't know if it makes any difference, but—'

The phone rang again.

Tasha stretched out her hand and pushed a lock of hair
out of his face. 'Chaz,' she said, 'I know you don't like me
to tell you it was wonderful.' She gave him a mischievous
smile. 'But it looks as though that thing you said was right.'

The phone rang.

'That thing I said?'

'You said we were obviously meant for each other,' she
said. 'At a purely physical level.' Her hand was still in his
hair because it felt so good, so natural, so absolutely right
to be touching him. 'I know I was furious at the time, but
it's obviously true. It was—' she broke off, then went on,
her eyes brimming with amusement '—very, very, very,

very nice.' She smoothed his hair back, still smiling. 'You really don't have to apologise. But if there's something you want to tell me…' she let her hand slide down along the rough line of his jaw '…perhaps you should wait till after you've answered the phone.'

The phone rang one more time while he stared into her face. Then he shrugged and picked up the receiver.

There was a short pause.

'Toni?' he said blankly. There was another pause, followed by a torrent of French.

The conversation went on for a long time. Chaz was frowning. Every once in a while he would gesticulate in an idiomatic way to go along with all the incomprehensible idiomatic things he was saying. At last he moved back to shallow waters where Tasha was no longer out of her depth. 'You're where? Downstairs? Two minutes, OK? We've got to get dressed,' said Chaz.

He put down the receiver and smiled wryly at Tasha. 'So much for a day in bed. She seems to have had some kind of bust-up with Jean-Luc,' he said. 'As you can probably guess, she's never been exactly the soul of tact. She said he was never going to be any good and he got pretty violent and now she wants to go to New York.'

'What—today?' asked Tasha.

He grinned. 'Well, she always was one for burning her bridges before she'd crossed them.' He swung his feet over the side to the floor and sat up. 'She's half-American, though you'd never know—father walked out when she was two and she grew up here, but at least she doesn't need a visa. It's not as crazy as it sounds. And she's right about one thing—Paris is a dead end for her right now. And quite possibly dangerous.'

He ran an impatient hand through his hair. 'The French side of her family are pretty well off, though again you'd never know to look at her, but they washed their hands of her years ago. She doesn't really have anyone to turn to. I'd better see what I can do for her.'

'Of course,' said Tasha. 'What was it you wanted to say to me?'

'Oh—' said Chaz. He hesitated, then shrugged. 'It'll keep. We'd better get going. You can have the shower first if you like.'

Tasha showered rapidly, then disappeared into her own room to change. She heard the shower start up again, then stop, then the sound of his door opening again. It seemed only a couple of seconds before she heard a loud knock on his door from the corridor.

She went to her own door and opened it. 'I'm afraid he's still dressing,' she began.

Toni turned a ravaged face to her. She was still wearing her clothes from the night before, but the kohl round her eyes was streaked with tears.

Chaz's door opened. He had on trousers and an open-necked shirt, but his feet were bare, his hair was wet and he still needed a shave.

'Chaz,' sobbed Toni, throwing herself into his arms.

'It's all right,' said Chaz. 'Let's go into Tasha's room; it's a bit more presentable.'

He escorted her into Tasha's room, an arm round her shoulders, and led her to sit on a small love-seat. Toni was gulping out her story, in English now; Chaz was making soothing noises.

Tasha sat on the bed, fighting down irritation. When *she* had been at her lowest ebb all Chaz had been able to do was make sarcastic remarks. *Now* look at him. He had taken out a handkerchief and was wiping away the tears, an expression of sympathy and concern on his usually mocking face. Instead of teasing the girl he was murmuring something comforting. Well, all right, Chaz had been quite nice to Tasha on occasion, but there was always that mockery in the background.

Chaz was saying, 'No, look, it's no problem. We'll see if we can get you on the flight. If not we'll stay over an extra day.'

Instead of making a polite protest Toni just gave him a brave grin, then leant her head on his shoulder.

'Thank you, Chaz,' she said, with that lovely French accent making the English words sound better than any native speaker ever could. She raised her head again to look in his eyes. 'I knew I could count on you,' she said.

Tasha scowled. The honeymoon was over.

# CHAPTER SEVEN

THE next two weeks reminded Tasha, oddly, of the days before her wedding. Once again Chaz had decided to play the knight errant—a workaholic knight errant in overdrive. Within an hour of wiping Toni's tear-streaked face with his handkerchief he had got her a first-class seat on their flight to New York and made arrangements for someone to collect her things from her flat. By the time they'd caught their plane he had grilled the young singer on the work she'd been doing since he'd seen her last, made half a dozen phone calls to clubs that might have openings, and lined up five auditions and a 'We'll see'. By the time they'd got off the plane he had made another twenty or thirty phone calls to people in the music business.

Tasha had always wondered whether anyone actually used the credit-card activated phones installed in the seat backs. She'd always wondered how anyone could talk for more than two seconds on such a phone without having a heart attack at the prospective bill. Chaz, however, had seemed perfectly happy to have expansive conversations that went, 'How've you been, you old so and so,' for about five minutes before getting to the point. It had taken her a while to realise that calling from the plane was part of the point. It had gotten worked casually into every single conversation, so that by the time they'd got off the plane twenty or thirty people in the music business had known that somebody hot was coming into town, and if they were lucky they could get her first.

By the end of the first week Toni had had her first ap-

pearance in a club. And by the end of the second week she
had taken the town by storm.

The club she had opened in was packed night after night
on the basis of word of mouth alone. Rave reviews followed. Agents fought to represent her, clubs fought to book
her, record companies fought to sign her. And Tasha had
watched it all happen.

She knew, of course, that Toni couldn't have succeeded
if she hadn't had genuine talent. Tasha could still remember
the rough, sweet voice drifting out over the Seine, throwing
the old song round its shoulders like a secondhand coat
from a flea market. Toni had had star quality even then,
and she'd drawn in the crowds when she was just a nobody.
But New York was the most competitive city in the world.
There were singers just as talented waiting on tables and
tending bar, waiting for a break that never came.

Chaz had made it all happen, and because it had happened so fast he had made it look easy. But Tasha knew
from her own experiences in the book trade that it wasn't
easy at all. It had taken not only the shrewd intelligence
and lazy charm which were the attractive side of his character, but also the cool cynicism and bulldozing ruthless-
ness which had always infuriated her—all those, and a track
record which had made people in one of the most cut-throat
businesses in the world drop everything when he'd said,
'Listen to this'.

In a way, of course, there was nothing in all this that she
didn't know already. But knowing it was different from
seeing it firsthand. Tasha began to feel, grudgingly, that
she'd been too ready to condemn Chaz out of hand over
the years. She'd held it against him that he'd been unfail-
ingly exasperating in the small pond of family life. Well,
she hadn't been wrong in one sense—he *had* been infuriating. But it was a bit like criticising a ship that was built
for the open sea for not fitting in a bathtub.

Seeing Chaz for the first time in his element, she felt as if she were somehow seeing him for the first time. Reluctantly, she had to admit there was something dangerously attractive even in the things she'd disliked. There was also, unfortunately, something dangerously attractive in all the things she'd *always* recognised as attractive. His dark, piratical good looks were, if anything, more potent now that she'd slept with him. The slightest flicker of a hooked eyebrow, the faintest curve of the firm mouth, an absentminded tapping of a pencil with those long, clever fingers—the most trivial physical details could fill her with awareness, reminding her of the way he had looked at her, the way he had kissed her, the way he had touched her. Terrifyingly, unbelievably, Tasha was beginning to think Bad Cousin Chaz might actually be her type.

Which was too bad, since it was obvious that she wasn't his.

She'd been nervous about the awkwardness of living alone with him, but she needn't have worried—they hadn't *been* alone. Chaz had invited Toni to stay with them until she found a place of her own. Most of the time Chaz had been busy chasing down anyone who could be useful; at night they'd gone to hear Toni's show, then on to parties where Chaz would chase down contacts with such panache all the people who hadn't been chased had felt left out. They'd stay until the small hours of the morning to give Toni a chance to come on from the club; a frisson of excitement would run through the party, and they'd leave in half an hour.

In the taxi Chaz and Toni would argue and make rude jokes and swap irreverent comments on all the people who'd tried to impress them, sometimes in machine-gun French, sometimes in Toni's idiomatic English. It was only too obvious they were two of a kind, with an effortless rapport that all the insults they traded couldn't conceal.

They'd get back to the flat and Toni would throw herself on a sofa, still talking a hundred miles an hour. Just sprawling on the sofa she had a lazy animal grace, the sensuality of someone absolutely at ease with herself physically—a sensuality that Tasha found oddly familiar until she realised why. Chaz had it too.

He'd pull Tasha down beside him on another sofa and lean lazily back, an arm around her shoulders, while he carried on his post mortem of the party with Toni. Tasha would lean self-consciously back too, embarrassed to separate herself too obviously, nervous of giving in to the strong physical attraction which he exerted so unthinkingly even when his attention was on somebody else. She would feel Toni looking at her, wondering what on earth Chaz had seen in her, wondering how he'd ended up with someone so talentless and repressed and boring as a wife.

Finally Toni would say, 'Well, I better let you lovebirds get to bed,' with a mocking look. She'd spring to her feet, stride over to Chaz, kiss him on the cheek, or on the mouth if she happened to feel like it, and saunter off to her bedroom.

Then Chaz would give Tasha a rueful grin and say something offhand. 'See you in my dreams,' he'd say, with one of those easy, charming smiles. 'Any time you change your mind you've only to say the word,' he'd say smiling, not saying anything to try to make her change her mind, not touching her or kissing her or doing any of the hundred things he'd done on the honeymoon to make her change her mind. 'If you wake up in the middle of a wet towel, wet T-shirt sort of dream and want the real thing you know where to find me,' he'd say, with a wry grin, just as if he hadn't broken all his promises to stay at arm's length again and again when he'd really wanted her.

Then he'd kiss her on the cheek, spring to his feet, and stride off to his own bedroom without a backward look.

And night after night Tasha would trail back to her own room, arguing furiously with herself. She didn't *want* to be involved with Chaz. It was just injured vanity. He was being nicer than she'd expected, but basically she was now finished business. He'd once joked about how he'd give her the perfect excuse for divorce if he committed adultery within a month of the wedding; well, any day now he'd get on with it. He was keeping up the pretence of the marriage for Toni's benefit—to do him justice, he obviously didn't want to humiliate Tasha by starting an affair in what was now her own home. But once Toni found a place of her own it would be just a matter of time.

As the days went on Tasha felt more and more edgy. It would almost be a relief when the inevitable happened. At least there would be no more of this pretence; at least she wouldn't go on wondering when the axe was going to fall. It wasn't as if she was emotionally involved, after all. She was attracted to him. It would hurt her pride, a little, for everyone in New York to know how soon Chaz had moved on to someone else—but then, considering the competition, they were probably surprised he hadn't already. Once it happened she could stop thinking about it and get on with her own life.

In the meantime she was finding it harder and harder to sleep. She would go to bed with her cheek tingling from his goodnight kiss, and she would lie there remembering her honeymoon, which in retrospect seemed one long non-stop orgy. She knew it hadn't really been like that, but she was remembering the highlights. How simple things had been in the days when Chaz would just wander into her room in a wet towel. How simple things had been in the days when she'd dragged him through the Louvre for hours on end without once quenching that lurking smile in his eyes.

Tasha would go to bed at five o'clock, or six, and lie

in bed punching her pillow, remembering how simple things had been, until she woke up at noon, or eleven, or ten... By the end of their third week in New York Toni still hadn't had time to find an apartment; Tasha went to bed at five-thirty, and woke up, knowing she would not sleep again, at seven.

She scowled into the dim dawn-lit room. How much longer was this going to go on? Maybe she should just find an apartment for herself and leave Chaz and Toni to fall into each other's arms.

She threw back the covers and leapt impatiently out of bed. She was *not* going to lie here wasting mental energy on this. If they wanted to sleep together, let them. She had better things to think about. She was going to get up, have a cup of coffee, and see if she couldn't remember what they were.

She stalked barefooted through the palatial apartment, her feet sinking into the thick soft rugs which covered its floors. As she neared the kitchen, her nose was tantalised by the scent of fresh coffee.

She padded into the immense white room and found Chaz sitting on a stool, a steaming mug between his hands. His hair was wet; he had shaved; he was dressed.

Tasha stared at him. He'd been working eighteen and twenty-hour days ever since they'd got back, the endless rounds of parties being as much work as the endless phone calls. He'd gone to bed at the same time she had. He must have spent even less time there than she had if he'd managed to shower, shave and dress within an hour and a half.

'Chaz?' she said doubtfully.

His face lit with the charming, easy smile he'd given her so often since they'd arrived. 'Tasha? What a nice surprise.'

'I couldn't sleep,' she said. 'I—was a bit on edge for some reason.'

'Same here,' he said. 'I thought I'd come out here and listen to the radio.'

She hadn't even noticed that the radio was on, but she now realised that she should have been surprised that he had just been sitting there, without even a paper to read.

'WQBQ,' he explained. 'That station I was thinking of buying. Thought I'd see what the new owners are doing with it.'

Tasha had heard a lot about WQBQ since arriving in New York. Whenever the scary, successful people she'd met at parties had not been raving about Chaz's latest discovery they'd been complaining bitterly because he had allowed the cult station to be bought by someone who didn't understand it. People would demand an explanation and Chaz would shrug and say he'd decided it wasn't for him. He'd never shown any sign of having regrets, but maybe he was having second thoughts.

'After a good hour's sleep,' she said.

Chaz shrugged. 'You know how it is; you get so wound up you can't wind down. Things should calm down once Toni's agent takes things in hand. She can move out without feeling she's leaving general headquarters behind.'

'It's wonderful what you've done for her,' said Tasha.

'I couldn't have done much if she hadn't had the talent,' he said with a shrug. 'I hope you haven't felt too neglected. It wasn't the way I pictured introducing you to New York, but it was one of those make-or-break situations—it wouldn't have done her any good to hang about waiting to get noticed. I know I haven't had much time for you.'

'Oh, no, it's fine,' said Tasha. 'It's been interesting to watch you,' she added politely. She took a mug off a hook and poured herself a coffee.

Chaz gave a crack of laughter. 'That sounds ominous,' he said.

'No, really,' said Tasha. She jumped up on the stool next

to his. 'I know people throw around the words ''major talent'', but Toni's the real thing, isn't she?' she said, forcing herself to be generous. 'She deserves a break. If you didn't have a lot of, er, qualities that, er, tend to irritate people who are trying to have a nice quiet Sunday dinner with just the family, you probably couldn't be so, er, effective,' she said, stumbling through what amounted to a retraction of some two-thirds of the hard things she'd thought about him over the years.

One corner of his mouth had quirked up in a crooked smile as she began, then an eyebrow had shot up; by the time she'd finished his eyes were alight with laughter. 'Well, that was worth getting out of bed for,' he said. 'But you *have* had a sleepless night—I'd better not hold you to it.'

He was still smiling at her. On impulse, without stopping to think, she stretched out a hand to touch the silky, freshly shaven skin of his jaw.

His eyes held hers, suddenly intense. 'Better and better,' he said softly. 'Any chance of a good-morning kiss?'

Her heart seemed to be pounding at the base of her throat. It was hard to breathe. She didn't know whether she nodded, or leant towards him. He slipped off his stool and suddenly his arms were around her and his mouth was on hers and her mouth was locked against his. Oh, God, had it really been three weeks?

She lost track of time; she could not have said whether a few minutes or half an hour went by before he raised his head. 'Well, that was worth waiting for,' he said. His eyes were bright. 'And all for showing I can swim with the sharks. Who'd have guessed it?'

'I, er…' said Tasha.

'Shall we go back to bed?' he asked.

'Er…' said Tasha. It occurred to her that it had now been over six weeks since Chaz had proposed to her. Six weeks and he had only had sex once. He probably hadn't been celibate that long since leaving school. He was probably dying of frustration. He hadn't wanted to sleep with her enough to make any advances himself, but when she seemed ready to fall in his arms he wasn't above taking advantage of it.

Tasha suppressed a sigh. You couldn't just manufacture the kind of rapport Chaz had with Toni. The contrast between that, and his polite treatment of Tasha, had been staring her in the face ever since they arrived. Tasha couldn't imagine being in love with one person and coolly sleeping with someone else who happened to be available, but Chaz didn't seem to see anything out of the way about it. It was odd, but then men *were* odd.

'I'm sorry,' she said. 'I know this must be hard for you, Chaz.'

'Sorry?' he said.

'Going six weeks and only having sex once,' she said. 'I know you're not used to being celibate that long. It must be very frustrating.'

'Whereas it naturally isn't a problem for you,' said Chaz. 'Long live the double standard. I think I can hold out a *bit* longer if I absolutely have to.'

'I—I just meant—' she stammered.

'That it's different for girls,' he completed sardonically. 'You can take it or leave it, but you mostly leave it.'

What he meant, obviously, was that he thought she should be more like Toni, who would always go after any man she happened to want without a lot of soul-searching. What he meant was that she just wasn't his type. There was nothing she could say, though, that wouldn't sound like a request for reassurance.

'Look,' he said. 'Forget I said anything. I thought you might have changed your mind. It was a misunderstanding.

I read too much into it.' He smiled. 'Will you kiss me again
if I promise not to get the wrong idea?'

His face was level with hers. She bent forward and
brushed his mouth with hers. His mouth followed hers as
she drew away, taking another kiss. She laughed and put
her arms round his neck. He was wearing a suit and tie,
presumably for a business meeting later on, but she was
still in her pyjamas; she could feel his hands on her waist
through the thin cotton. She had a sudden, vivid memory
of the touch of his hands on her bare skin. His mouth was
lingering on hers—he wasn't kissing her as if she were
second best.

A thought came to her, as sudden and vivid and seductive as the memory. Chaz was actually her *husband*. She
could go back to his bedroom and wreak havoc with what
the well-dressed businessman was wearing and do what
thousands of husbands and wives did every day, and no
do anything that anyone would hold against her.

Toni was in love with Chaz, but she knew he was married to someone else—she accepted the fact that someone
else had the right to share his bed. Chaz was rediscovering
his love for Toni; he'd once said if he found the right
woman he'd forsake all others, but he seemed to have
changed his mind. Tasha could have a repeat of the last
night of her honeymoon with someone whose heart didn't
belong to her. If his kisses were anything to go by, it would
be just as spectacular physically as last time. And from a
purely legalistic point of view it wouldn't be wrong.
Adultery would be Chaz sleeping with someone he loved.
It wouldn't be Chaz sleeping with the wife he didn't care
about.

With a superhuman effort of will-power Tasha forced
herself to pull her head away. She unlocked her arms from
behind his neck, drawing them back towards her until her
hands rested on his shoulders, holding him away from her

Just looking at his mouth made her want to kiss it again. She gritted her teeth. She had to stop this now.

'That was lovely,' she said, struggling to get her breathing under control.

Chaz was giving her another of his sardonic looks. Well, too bad.

'Oh, Chaz, I've wrinkled your tie,' she added artlessly. 'Let me straighten it for you.'

She smoothed out the dark red silk and tightened the crisp knot.

'My God, you're cool,' he said. He raised an eyebrow. 'Well, at least I'm not likely to get the wrong idea. Party's over.'

Tasha smiled at him. 'It was really lovely, Chaz,' she assured him. 'Just like our honeymoon.'

'Yes,' he agreed. 'Just like all the bits I was trying to forget.'

'Oh,' said Tasha. 'Does that mean you didn't enjoy it?'

'No,' said Chaz. 'That's not what I meant.'

He was looking into her face with a mixture of exasperation and something else she couldn't place. Suddenly his eyes shifted to a point just behind her.

'Good morning, you two,' said Toni, in a voice even huskier with sleep. 'So you do have a love life after all. I couldn't decide if I was giving you inhibitions or if you were maybe just being very quiet.'

She walked round the counter to pour herself a coffee. Tasha saw, to her surprise, that she was already dressed.

'I'm sorry if I've been in the way,' Toni added. 'I've found an apartment anyway. I didn't have time to tell you guys last night. The taxi is on his way to pick me up.' She grinned at Chaz. 'Come up and see me some time,' she said.

'You haven't been in the way,' he said. 'And of course I'll come and see you.'

'You've been great,' said Toni. 'I won't forget it.'

The buzzer from downstairs sounded by the kitchen door. Chaz pressed a button. The voice of the doorman crackled through to announce Toni's taxi.

'You can carry my stuff to the elevator,' said Toni.

Chaz grinned and said something in French that sounded distinctly impolite. He picked up a couple of bags, a bird-cage and a hatbox that Toni had left by the door. He left the room followed by Toni, who had her ghetto-blaster on her shoulder and a pair of rollerblades under her arm.

Tasha hesitated. It didn't seem right to let Toni leave without saying goodbye; on the other hand Toni probably didn't want her around when she said goodbye to Chaz.

After a couple of minutes of agonising Tasha followed them. She reached the door and stood stock still.

Toni and Chaz stood in the hall, bags, cage, hatbox, ghetto-blaster and skates on the floor at their feet. Toni put her hands on Chaz's shoulders and stood on tiptoe; she gave him a long, searingly erotic kiss.

She dropped back to stand flat-footed, and said something rapid and urgent in French, the black-rimmed eyes staring up at him.

Chaz said something equally incomprehensible. He flicked her cheek with a finger.

'Any time you get tired of being married you know where to find me,' said Toni, switching to English, as if she knew that her accent made the words as erotic as the kiss.

Chaz hesitated, looking down at her.

'If I get tired of being married, I'll let you know,' he said at last.

# CHAPTER EIGHT

TASHA crept silently back to the kitchen. She hadn't discovered anything she didn't already know, but she had a sore, miserable feeling inside, as if in spite of what she knew she had believed the look in his eyes, believed she wasn't second best. It was stupid to feel sore and miserable about the passing of a brief relationship that had, after all, been based only on physical attraction. She knew it was stupid, but she felt it anyway.

She knew it would only make her feel worse to know for certain that Chaz wanted to end the marriage, as he obviously did, but she had to know anyway. She didn't want Chaz to think she'd been spying on them, though, so she did not raise the subject when he came back to the kitchen and found her drinking her coffee. She waited until he came home that evening.

She had put on a narrow, silver-green silk dress which went with her eyes as a feeble morale-booster: she did not want to look completely pathetic. And just for a moment she thought she must have misunderstood the scene at the door. Chaz got home at seven and took one look at her and his eyes lit up in a way that reminded her of Paris, when he hadn't been able to stop looking at her.

'Alone at last,' he said smiling. 'You look lovely, Tash. What say we go out to dinner, just the two of us?'

'If you like,' she said, smiling up at him; just the warmth in his eyes made it impossible not to smile.

'I like if you like,' he said.

He was looking at her the way he once had when he had said she could take him through Paris brick by brick and

135

he would still want her. It hardly seemed necessary to ask the question that had been gnawing at her all day, but after all it wasn't really fair not to ask it.

'Chaz,' she said.

'Tasha?'

'If you ever decide this isn't working, you know you only have to say,' she said. 'I mean, if you decide for some reason that you want a divorce before the end of the year...' She trailed off as all the warmth drained from his face.

'Is this because of this morning?' he asked.

'This morning?' she said nervously, wondering if he'd guessed that she'd overheard.

'Look,' he said. 'I'm sorry I jumped the gun. It won't happen again. We agreed that what happened in Paris wouldn't happen again, and it won't.'

Tasha looked at him blankly. 'That's not what I meant,' she said. 'I just meant that if *you* thought it wasn't working you should say.' She smiled at him. 'It wasn't because you kissed me. It was really lovely.'

Surely now he would smile at her again, and perhaps even kiss her again. Unless she was right after all, and he was in love with Toni...

Chaz just gave her a sardonic look. 'How lovely,' he said. 'Well, in that case I don't see much point in getting divorced, do you?'

Tasha had thought he would either accept her offer or insist that he was happy with the present arrangement, and that either way would put her out of her uncertainty. But she felt just as much at a loss as she had before. The next few weeks did nothing to clear matters up.

Things were quieter now that Toni was gone, but they had not gone back to the easy camaraderie of their second week in Paris. Chaz had dropped even the pretence that they were a couple in private. Instead of putting his arm

round her shoulders he'd watch the news perched on the
arm of a chair, or sitting on the sofa, legs outstretched, a
good three feet away from her. He'd stopped saying that if
she changed her mind she had only to say the word. In
other words, everything was exactly the way she'd *wanted*
it to be when she'd accepted his proposal, except that now
it left her with that stupid sore, miserable feeling that would
not go away.

Chaz insisted on going to Toni's show every night, just
as if the hottest item in New York needed moral support.
Toni sang her heartbreaking songs in a packed club instead
of on a bridge, but she still seemed to be singing them for
one person only. Looking at the grim face of the man beside her, Tasha could tell it was tearing him apart. So why
didn't he just *tell* her? Instead he kept her at arm's length,
pricking her with mocking remarks whenever she looked
as if she was coming too close.

Then one night their uneasy skirmishes escalated into
war.

They started at a drinks party, then went to a gallery
opening, and finally reached a 'party' party at about eleven.
As usual wherever they went people converged on Chaz as
soon as they entered the room. Tasha saw a few people she
knew and tried to talk to them, with about her usual success—people could talk of nothing but Chaz and Toni. By
the time they reached the last party she was feeling slightly
shell shocked.

Chaz was swept away by a crowd of sophisticated strangers. Toni arrived late and gravitated automatically to his
side; everyone around them was talking excitedly.

Suddenly, across the room, Tasha saw a painting on the
wall which had recently sold for a record-breaking price. It
was a painting by Cézanne which she'd seen in dozens of
art books, and here it was in a private home, completely
ignored by everyone.

Tasha slipped through the crowd. It was a still life; there was a glowing deep green pear, a peach that glowed red. Her first thought was that she had never seen anything so beautiful; her second was that looking at the picture would be a perfectly acceptable reason not to talk to anyone.

'It's beautiful, isn't it?' said a voice beside her.

She turned. A man was standing beside her. He had classically chiselled features, light brown hair, light blue eyes, and he was dressed with the expensive understatement which people liked here when they didn't want to be totally outrageous.

He smiled at her. '''Full many a flower is born to blush unseen'',' he said, 'but it's kind of shocking when it goes unseen in a room full of people.'

Tasha smiled shyly back. 'I know,' she said. 'It's amazing to think someone could have something like this in their home.'

He shrugged. 'Well, that's New York for you. You're English, aren't you?'

Tasha had been asked this question some two hundred times since her arrival, but she was willing to overlook this in someone who had taken pity on a wallflower. 'Yes,' she said. 'I'm Tasha Taggart, by the way. What's your name?'

'Phil Jones.' He shook hands with her. 'Tasha Taggart—you wouldn't by any chance be *Mrs* Taggart?'

'I'm married to Chaz Taggart, yes,' said Tasha. She waited defensively for the blank look as he tried to work out how someone as insignificant as herself had beaten all the dazzling beauties Chaz had known over the years.

'Well, now that I've met you I understand everything,' he said, smiling. 'He's a lucky man.' He grinned. 'I was in half a mind not to come tonight, but I was going stir crazy in my apartment and I'd promised Mona I'd be here. I walk in the door, and what do you know? Virtue rewarded.'

Tasha supposed he was just being polite, but then nobody

else was even bothering to be polite. 'What do you do?' she asked.

He grimaced. 'I'm a publisher,' he said. 'At the moment, a spectacularly unsuccessful one, and New York, as you've probably worked out by now, doesn't have a lot of time for the unsuccessful. I publish art books, some fiction—things a little ahead of their time.' The blue eyes met hers. 'You have to make enough of a market to at least stay in the black, and you're walking a pretty fine line. It's hard to get it right, and I had the bad luck to get it wrong.'

Tasha smiled up at him. 'I'm so sorry,' she said. 'But it must be wonderful to know you're doing something worth doing. I'd love to see some of your books. Why don't you give me a list of your favourites? Then I'll keep an eye out for them the next time I'm in a bookstore.' She grinned. 'At least it'll give you a bit more on the credit side of the ledger!'

He gave her a rather strained smile. 'That's very kind of you,' he said. 'But I'm afraid I'll never see any of the money; it'll go straight to my creditors. When I said spectacularly unsuccessful I wasn't exaggerating; the company went bankrupt last month.'

'I'm—I'm so sorry,' stammered Tasha. She'd always heard that bankruptcy meant something rather different in America—he looked exactly like all the other rich people in the room.

He shrugged. 'It's an odd feeling. The worst has happened, your life has come crashing down around your ears, but everything goes on just the same. *You* go on just the same, going to parties you got invitations for before people knew they probably weren't going to want to know you, and you turn up and you have the same conversations you had before, maybe you even go on talking about some talented writer you've discovered, just as if you were in a position to do something for him…'

Tasha stared at him, her grey-green eyes misty with sympathy. 'I know what you mean,' she said. 'I do know what you mean. But you mustn't give up. If you keep trying, I know it will work out.'

A slight movement of the group of people to her right suddenly gave her a clear view straight across the room. Chaz was standing in a crowd of about ten, who were all howling with laughter at something he'd said. Even from across the room she could see he was furious about something. His eyes were blazing with bad temper; just the set of his head said he'd like to murder somebody.

'Well, I hope you're right,' said Phil.

Tasha smiled. 'I'm sure of it,' she said.

She was about to make some other sympathetic, encouraging remark, but she didn't get the chance. Chaz broke suddenly away from his group and came striding through the room.

'Hello, Phil, thanks for looking after Tasha,' he said tightly.

'No thanks required,' Phil said easily. 'You're a lucky man.'

'I know,' said Chaz. The black eyes were sizzling. 'Too bad you went belly-up, Phil,' he added, in a drawling voice whose calculated rudeness was worse than the actual words. 'But it was bound to happen sooner or later. You've a rare talent for spotting pretentious mediocrity and bringing out the worst in it; it's not exactly surprising that you couldn't fool any of the people any of the time.'

Tasha stared at him in open-mouthed horror. *'Chaz!'* she said furiously. 'How *could* you?' She turned to Phil, who was looking white around the mouth. 'I'm terribly sorry,' she said. 'I'm sure he doesn't really mean it—'

Chaz broke in without apology. 'Ever seen any of his books, Tash?' he asked, raising an eyebrow.

'No, but—'

'Then how can you be so bloody sure I can't mean it? Tell you what, I'll have a trawl through the remainder shops, see if I can find any that haven't been pulped, and you can have a look through them and show me the error of my ways.' The drawling voice was, if anything, worse this time than the last.

Tasha took in the hard black eyes, the sardonic lifted eyebrow, the sneering mouth. This was not a man who was about to apologise and say, I'm sorry if I hurt your feelings. This was a man who had found himself living with the wrong woman just when he'd rediscovered the love of his life; he'd been frustrated for weeks and was positively spoiling for a fight. As long as they stood there Chaz was going to go on, not so much hurling insults as taking careful aim and scoring one perfect bull's-eye after another.

Tasha looked up at him, her misty eyes for once as hard as stone. 'Chaz,' she said icily. 'Is there anyone else you want to talk to at this party?'

'No.'

'Then let's go.'

'Must we?' said Chaz. 'I was just starting to enjoy myself. Wonderful to see you again anyway, Phil, sorry to cut it short but that's married life for you; your time isn't your own.'

Tasha realised he was probably searching for some particularly devastating parting shot. Well, maybe it wouldn't be quite so humiliating for Phil without an audience.

She turned on her heel and stalked away from them. People were murmuring and watching but she ignored them, heading straight for the door.

Chaz caught up with her easily.

'You didn't say goodbye to Phil,' he said reproachfully. 'That wasn't very polite, Tash.'

'I don't want to talk to you,' said Tasha.

Chaz took out his mobile phone, keyed in a few numbers,

and told his driver to meet them at the door. 'It's all right, darling, I said goodbye for us both,' he told her. 'I wished him luck in his new career, whatever that might be. He's certainly going to need it.'

Tasha did not reply. She maintained a stony silence all the way down from the penthouse to the ground floor; she maintained a stony silence as they got into the car; she maintained a stony silence during the drive home and the ascent to the twentieth floor.

When they got into the penthouse, however, she turned on him in fury.

'How *could* you, Chaz?' she blazed. 'How could you deliberately *savage* someone who was at rock bottom?'

He flicked an eyebrow up. 'Seemed a good idea at the time, Tash,' he said coolly. 'Irresistible impulse. Anything else you want to talk about? If not I think I'll retire for the evening and read Spinoza.'

He'd thrust his hands in his pockets and was already walking away from her.

Tasha stalked up to him. *'No!'* she said furiously. 'Don't you *dare* walk away from me.' Chaz ignored this, so she walked around and stood in front of him, looking up into his face.

'If you *had* to be rude to someone,' she said, 'you had a whole *roomful* of rich, successful people to pick on. So why out of all those people did you have to pick the *one person* who was just trying to pick himself up off the ground? How could you *do* such a thing?'

Chaz stood looking down at her with an impenetrable expression. He said at last, 'All right, Tash, I'll tell you if you really want to know.'

'Well?' said Tasha.

He shrugged. 'I took you to a party with, as you say, a whole roomful of people who were making a success of things one way or another. They work in the most competitive city in the world, and, yes, it does make them cynical and ruthless and sometimes superficial, but for God's sake, Tash, there's a lot of talent there too, and I thought you'd have a marvellous time.'

He raised an eyebrow. 'Well, I turn my back for two minutes, and the next thing I know I find you've managed to locate, with *unerring* instinct, the one out-and-out loser in the place, somebody whose idea of a brilliant book is to print on facing pages a reproduction of a Van Gogh and a reproduction of a postcard of the picture, because somebody told him it would be so post-modern and he thought it would make him a lot of money.'

Tasha frowned. 'Yes, but even if it *wasn't* a good idea you don't have to be gratuitously rude,' she said. 'And I didn't *locate* him. I went over to look at the Cézanne because nobody was talking to me, and he came up and he was terribly nice.'

Chaz struck his head with his hand. 'You're not listening to me,' he said. 'You're not listening to yourself. You'd been introduced to some people; why didn't *you* go and talk to *them*?'

'Because they terrify me,' Tasha said frankly. There was no point pretending otherwise, but she could not help stiffening defensively. It was only too obvious that what he looked for in a woman was something she could never be: someone like Toni, who wouldn't *let* herself be ignored.

'That's exactly what I mean,' he said in exasperation. 'You underestimate yourself to the point where you think nobody who has anything to offer can possibly be interested in you. Then you back off into a corner, some no-hoper comes up and tells you a sob story and you take common cause with him because you know what it feels like to be left out.'

He thrust his hand back in his pocket and began pacing

up and down, shooting furious glances at her from the crackling black eyes.

'The difference is you don't have to be left out. For some reason, which I can't for the life of me make out, you feel happier standing in a corner being sympathetic to someone who thinks life owes him a free ride. The only thing I can think is, maybe you feel better being around people who don't offer any competition to you or anyone else; maybe it bolsters your self-esteem to talk to someone who *needs* your sympathy.'

'That's not true!' Tasha said hotly.

'No?' He raised a sceptical eyebrow. 'If I hadn't stepped in you'd probably be well on your way to filling Jeremy's shoes with a suitable replacement. Phil's been living off various well-meaning female relations for years; seems the well has run dry and he's probably looking for alternative sources of subsidy.'

Tasha closed her eyes for a moment. Was Chaz actually insane? How long had she talked to Phil anyway? Five minutes? And Chaz was already identifying him as a love interest?

'Chaz,' she said impatiently. 'Could I just point out that I talked to him for a maximum of five minutes? He's quite good-looking, obviously, but I wasn't *attracted* to him...'

'That's never stopped you in the past,' he said drily.

'Besides, nobody here knows anything about me. So even if he *does* have more than friendship in mind, at least he can't be after Daddy's money.'

'No,' said Chaz even more drily. 'He's after mine.'

Tasha gasped. *'What?'* she said incredulously. 'That's a *horrible* thing to say.'

He shrugged. 'But realistic. He's in serious financial difficulties, Tash. He's not in a position to be too choosy about his methods.'

Tasha thought again of the engaging man at the party.

He certainly hadn't seemed like the mercenary adventurer of Chaz's overactive imagination.

'I think you're imagining things, Chaz,' she said wearily. 'You're so cynical you think everyone else is like you.'

Chaz stopped dead in his tracks. 'Whatever my faults, I don't go around looking for a woman to pay my way,' he said. 'I don't think I would if things went wrong, but the fact is I've never had to find out.' An eyebrow swooped up in sudden self-mockery. 'You know, when I was in my teens I used to come across those profiles of successful businessmen. "I've never failed at anything I set out to do", they'd say, and I'd think, God, what a pompous ass. Well, here I am, Tash, I'm thirty-one and I've tried a lot of different things and every single one has come up trumps. It's partly just being in the right place at the right time, partly not liking to lose and being prepared to do whatever it takes to win—and the rest is pure genius.'

His eyes held hers. 'I'll never have any claims on your sympathy, Tash. I've always done exactly what I wanted; I've achieved everything I ever set out to do, and I can't even say it's been a disappointment when I got it. Funny thing is, I think you find that kind of track record a complete turn-off. Well, you might want to ask yourself why you consistently steer clear of anyone who doesn't need your sympathy.'

Tasha thought this was completely unfair. It wasn't her fault her boyfriends had always turned out to be needing someone to rely on.

'It's not your success I find unattractive, Chaz,' she said dampeningly. 'It's your habit of going for the jugular if someone happens to annoy you by not being as dazzlingly intelligent, handsome and successful as you are. I think the way you behaved to Phil was inexcusable, and I think you've completely misjudged him.'

Chaz shrugged. 'Well, we'll soon find out,' he said. 'I

suppose you'd think it was in bad taste to have a bet on it, but my guess is you'll hear from him by the end of the week—probably tomorrow.'

A thought struck him. He laughed suddenly. 'Tell you what, Tash, I'll show you my heart is in the right place— if I'm wrong I'll make it up to him. Let's see, I don't suppose his debts came to more than a quarter of a million; if he paid off the creditors as a gesture of goodwill he could re-establish his credit rating and start off with a clean slate. If he's as nice and ill-used as you say he deserves my support.'

He went to a desk at the side of the room and took out a chequebook. 'Pay-off number one,' said Chaz, scrawling something. 'One hundred thousand dollars, made payable to Mr Philip Jones; if he doesn't call you by the end of the week, it's his.'

*'What?'* said Tasha.

'Two,' said Chaz, scrawling again. 'One hundred thousand dollars if he hasn't asked you to ask me for money by the end of your third date.'

'What date?' said Tasha.

'Three,' said Chaz, dashing off another cheque. 'One hundred thousand dollars if he doesn't make a pass at you by the end of the month.' He paused, considering. 'Sorry, that's a bit vague. Let's say, if he hasn't asked you to do the kind of thing you promised not to do with anyone but me when we exchanged our vows.' He put the three slips of paper in an envelope and sealed it.

Tasha scowled at him. 'Chaz, you just can't do this,' she said. 'It's horrible.'

He flicked up an eyebrow. 'Not at all. If I'm wrong the least I owe him is an apology; rather quixotically, I'm offering him the chance to put his life back together instead. If I'm not wrong, I don't know that I'd say what he has in mind is horrible, but it's not very nice. On the other hand,

it can't be horrible of me to be right about it, and, as I was
saying just now, time will tell.'

A smile tugged at his mouth. 'Let me know what happens, Tash. I'm relying on your honour as a gentleman to
tell the truth.'

Tasha would have liked to take the envelope and tear it
up on the spot, but of course she couldn't do that. She had
no reason to think Phil had any ulterior motive in talking
to her; she couldn't just throw away a cool three hundred
thousand dollars of what would be in effect his money.

'Well, if you want to throw away three hundred thousand
dollars, who am I to stop you?' she said coolly.

'That's the girl.' He put the envelope in a drawer, and
closed it. 'I think the party at the Rosenbergs starts at eight;
if I have George pick you up at nine will that give you
enough time?' He seemed to regard the entire subject as
closed.

'I don't think I'll go,' said Tasha. The misty green eyes
met his steadily. 'I can see you thought this was just a
tempest in a teapot, Chaz, but I don't like it. I don't want
to go to parties wondering whether you're about to make
a scene because I haven't been nice enough to the right
people and I've been too nice to the wrong people. Maybe
if I'm not there you'll be able to behave yourself.'

To her annoyance he didn't even look slightly annoyed.
He gave a shout of laughter. 'Is that what they call tough
love, darling?' he said, grinning. 'Or just tough luck?'

He gave her the crooked smile that always disarmed her.
This time it just annoyed her. Apparently savaging an innocent bystander had been the one thing wanting to restore
him to good spirits. That, and the chance to play dog in the
manger. He hadn't shown any interest in her in weeks—as
soon as he'd thought someone else had, he'd had to estab-
lish ownership again.

'You've behaved inexcusably,' she said, sounding priggish even to herself. 'I don't know what it takes to make you see reason,' she added acidly, 'but since I don't seem to have succeeded maybe Spinoza will have better luck.' She gave him a rather malicious smile. 'I hope you find him entertaining,' she said as a parting shot, and she stalked out of the room.

# CHAPTER NINE

CHAZ left for the office the next day at eight. Tasha ate a leisurely breakfast, desultorily reading the *New York Times*. At ten the telephone rang.

Tasha picked up the receiver. 'Hello?' she said, hastily swallowing a mouthful of toast.

'Is that Tasha Taggart?'

'Yes?'

'This is Phil Jones; we met last night,' said the voice at the other end.

'Hello, Phil,' said Tasha with a sinking heart.

'I just called to see if you were all right last night. I hope you weren't too upset by what happened. People in New York can come across as pretty abrasive, and Taggart has lived here so long he's gone native.' He laughed at his own joke. 'I just wanted you to know I'm still in one piece.' He hesitated. 'And also to say how much I enjoyed our conversation.' He laughed again. 'To tell the truth, I didn't think of Taggart at all when I went home; all I could think of was you and how encouraging you'd been. You're right, of course, I should just pick myself up and move on.'

'Of course you should,' said Tasha. If he'd just set about picking himself up instead of calling her to *talk* about it, she thought, he could have had three hundred thousand dollars to help him move on. Well, he'd obviously seen how upset she'd been; it was nice of him to call to reassure her. Just because he'd called it didn't mean Chaz was right about the rest, so Phil could still have the two hundred thousand…

'Actually, I was wondering if you'd come and have

149

lunch with me,' said Phil. 'I know I don't have any right to ask it, but just talking to you last night made me feel better than I have for a long time. If you wouldn't mind meeting me I think it would really help me to start over.'

Tasha was about to agree automatically when a thought struck her. Her mouth curved up in a wicked smile. Two hundred thousand dollars would be an enormous help to Mr Jones, who had almost certainly been misjudged by her abominable cousin—but even if he *hadn't* been misjudged paying over the money would be acutely annoying for Chaz. Well, serve him right for being rude first and asking questions after. All she had to do to win this attractive sum for poor Mr Jones was refuse to see him again.

'I think you underestimate yourself,' she said encouragingly. 'You really don't need anyone else to help you, Phil.'

'I know that's true,' said Phil, 'but it helps to hear you say it, which was why I was hoping you'd agree to lunch. I could bring some of the books if you're interested.'

'Of course I'm interested,' said Tasha. 'But I'm terribly busy just now…'

'You've only just got here,' said Phil, a half-humorous tone just masking annoyance. 'You can't possibly be booked for lunch from here to Christmas.'

'No, of course not,' Tasha said desperately. 'But I just don't think it's a very good idea.'

'I see,' Phil said quietly. 'Well, obviously I'm not going to press you. I probably just got the wrong idea.'

'It's not that,' Tasha said defensively. 'It's just that—'

'Has he forbidden you to see me?' he asked. 'The overbearing *tyrant*!'

Tasha felt a spurt of temper. This was someone she'd talked to for five minutes, she thought indignantly. *He* didn't know her marriage wasn't for real; what right did he have to be criticising Chaz to her? If he wanted his two hundred thousand dollars, let him earn it.

'No, of course he hasn't forbidden me to see you,' she said. In fact, she thought acidly, Chaz would probably be overjoyed by the news. 'It's just a bit sudden. But of course I'd be happy to have lunch with you. Should we do something cheap? Maybe buy hot dogs in Central Park?'

There was a dumbfounded silence at the other end of the line. At last he said, 'But nobody who's anybody goes *there*, Tasha. I'll see if I can get us a table at Mario's. Is today all right for you?'

Tasha decided there was a silver lining in the cloud. At least Chaz wasn't here to hear this.

'Today's rather short notice,' she said carefully.

'Tomorrow, then? One o'clock?'

'Fine,' said Tasha. At least she could get it over with. Even if Chaz had misjudged Phil, she never wanted to see him again.

Tasha had planned to spend the evening enjoying several solid hours of American TV that was not three years out of date.

At eight the front door opened, and shut with a flourish.

'Honey, I'm home!' said Chaz, striding into the room and presenting her with a bouquet of roses with a dazzling smile.

'Aren't you going to the party?' asked Tasha, accepting the roses bemusedly.

'I decided I'd rather spend the evening quietly at home with you,' said Chaz. 'It will give me a chance to make real progress with Spinoza.'

'I'll just put these in water,' said Tasha, heading for the kitchen. Chaz followed her.

'How was your day?' he asked.

'Fine,' said Tasha, filling a vase with water.

'Any calls?'

Tasha gritted her teeth. 'Phil called,' she said.

Chaz gave a shout of laughter. 'Yess! Yesss! Remind me to tear up that cheque, will you?' His eyes were brimming with amusement.

Tasha dumped the roses in the vase. They really were lovely—there must have been about thirty of them, a glorious, dark velvety red with a sweet, fresh scent—but she was in no mood to appreciate them.

'He obviously realised how upset I was,' she said repressively.

'And wanted to show there were no hard feelings. How decent of him. Was that it?'

'We're having lunch tomorrow,' Tasha admitted reluctantly.

Chaz whistled. 'Quick work, Jones,' he said. He cocked an eyebrow. 'Is it just that you're irresistibly drawn to blonds, or hadn't it occurred to you that you could put a spoke in my wheel—and, of course, do him a good turn— by just saying no?'

Tasha glared at him. 'Believe me, I tried,' she said acerbically. 'But he wouldn't take no for an answer.'

Chaz laughed. 'Well, credit where credit's due, he's perseverant and hard-working. Wonder if he's ever thought of selling insurance policies?'

Tasha sighed. 'I'll try to remember to suggest it to him,' she said gloomily.

'Where's the big date?'

'We're meeting at Mario's at one.'

Chaz whistled again. 'Pretty high flying for a man who just went bust. Fancy a bet on who ends up paying for lunch?'

'Don't be ridiculous,' said Tasha. 'I suggested we have hot dogs in the park; this restaurant was his idea. He wouldn't suggest it if he couldn't afford it.'

'Want to bet?'

'No,' said Tasha. 'But only because I think it's in extremely bad taste. Thank you for the flowers. I'm going to watch TV. I know you want to read Spinoza, so I won't keep you.'

Chaz grinned at her. 'I can read Spinoza and watch *NYPD Blue* at the same time, darling. But if this is your way of saying you'd like to change the subject, your wish is my command. Just remember you're on your honour as a gentleman to tell me what happens at this lunch.'

Tasha wore a pale copper washed silk shift and glossy brown ankle boots to the lunch. She didn't want to wear anything that would look remotely as though it was meant to attract Phil. On the other hand, there was a limit to how far down she could dress if she was going to one of the most fashionable restaurants in town.

Phil was already waiting when she got to the restaurant. His blue eyes lit up when she came through the door.

'It's wonderful to see you again,' he said. 'I haven't been able to think of anything else all day.'

Tasha smiled politely. 'It's nice to see you again, too,' she lied.

'Well, let's go and sit down,' said Phil.

They were shown to a table in the middle of the floor.

Tasha started looking through the menu. The prices came as an unpleasant shock. Could Phil really afford this?

Phil overrode her insistence that she only wanted water to drink; he ordered a bottle of wine, and it wasn't just the house white. He then proceeded to order a lavish meal for himself. Tasha ordered soup and a salad.

Phil smiled. 'Well, as long as you're happy,' he said.

The wine came, and Phil raised his glass to her. 'To the best thing that's ever happened to me,' he said extravagantly.

The meal dragged on slowly. Phil explained his hopes and dreams, how it had all gone wrong, how wonderful it was to discover an artist or a writer with something to say, how wonderful it was to meet someone who understood that. Tasha just kept smiling sympathetically. The problem was, she was bored. She'd been married to Chaz two months; probably Phil was interesting enough in his way, but listening to him was like drinking flat ginger ale when you were used to champagne.

'I'm so sorry to hear that,' she said. 'How wonderful. What a shame. Oh, no! And then what did you say?'

Her attention drifted across the restaurant, across chattering groups, intent couples, the odd threesome, to a table near the window where a man was eating lunch. A black-haired, black-eyed, black-browed man...

Chaz raised his glass in mock salute.

Tasha glared at him.

'Is something the matter?' asked Phil.

'Oh, no, not at all,' said Tasha, schooling her features to one of courteous interest. 'What were you saying?'

'I was just telling you about this writer I've discovered.' The blue eyes met hers earnestly. 'You know, Tasha, I think this could be really big. Artistically important, but accessible too. I think this could be my big break and the hell of it is that financially I'm just not in a position to take advantage of it. I could do it for fifty thousand dollars— say sixty to cover all contingencies. That is, my lawyer would have to set up some kind of special framework because of my status, but obviously once it paid off that wouldn't be a problem...'

Tasha said desperately, 'It sounds very interesting, Phil, but, but, but—'

He hadn't actually *asked* for it yet; he'd just said what he could do with it if he had it. Tasha tried frantically to think of some way of stopping him. 'I need to go to the ladies' room!' she said at last.

'No, don't go yet.' He put a hand on her hand. 'Tasha—'

'Please don't say any more,' Tasha urged. *'Please.'*

'I've got to.' His eyes were bright. 'Tasha, you know how much this would mean to me. And not just to me—it's an important book. That kind of money is nothing to Taggart—'

Involuntarily her eyes drifted back to the man by the window. Now he wasn't alone. A familiar bleached head was facing him, leaning forward, gesturing furiously. The sardonic expression so familiar to Tasha was gone. Chaz was looking seriously, almost sombrely at Toni and shaking his head.

'Why don't you talk to him about it?' Tasha said feverishly, forcing herself to look away.

Phil made an impatient gesture. 'It would be a complete waste of time. He's got a knack for making money, of course, but he's a complete Philistine.'

Tasha bristled. 'He can't be a *complete* Philistine,' she said. 'He happens to be reading Spinoza.'

Phil shrugged. 'Whatever. It would just come so much better from you.' He gazed at her earnestly. 'Couldn't you approach him and persuade him to support the project?' he asked.

Tasha sighed. Some people just wouldn't *let* you help them. 'He wouldn't do it just on my say-so,' she said. She glanced back at the window in spite of herself. Chaz was holding Toni's hands in his.

Phil continued to argue the point. Tasha tried to listen, tried not to think about the couple at the other table, tried not to think about the stab of pain she'd felt at the look on Chaz's face as he held the singer's hands in his. Then there was a murmur in the restaurant. A chair was knocked over as someone stood up abruptly. Toni strode out of the restaurant, her face furious.

Phil glanced at the singer, then back at Tasha to pick up

the story—his own problems were obviously the only ones that mattered in the world.

Suddenly Phil broke off abruptly, looking up apprehensively. Tasha didn't have to ask why.

'Why, Tasha!' exclaimed a familiar voice three tables away. 'What an extraordinary coincidence! And Phil!' Tasha turned to find Chaz striding towards them, a look of unholy amusement on his face.

'Sorry about the other night, Phil,' Chaz said affably, coming to a halt by the table and looking down at them. 'My bark is worse than my bite.'

Phil muttered something noncommittal.

'I'm afraid I can't stop to chat,' said Chaz. 'Duty calls. I just wanted to ask Tasha whether I should tear up a couple of cheques.'

From the glint in his eye Tasha suspected he would have been only too happy to explain to his hapless victim. He'd obviously had some kind of show-down with Toni, and was yet again itching for a fight. 'Just two,' she said firmly.

Chaz raised an eyebrow. 'How disappointing,' he said. 'Ah, well, the day is still young. See you later, darling—I must fly.'

His departure cast a damper on the proceedings. Phil asked for the bill, and pulled a face when it came.

'Tasha,' he said apologetically. 'You're going to think I'm a total idiot, but I've come out without enough cash, and of course all my credit cards have been cancelled. Do you think you could bail me out, just temporarily?'

Tasha took out a credit card and gave it to the waiter without comment. Well, at least she wouldn't have to see Phil again. Escape was cheap at the price.

But as they left the restaurant Phil said impulsively, 'Tasha, why don't you at least come and see what I'm talking about? I don't live that far from here. Even if you really don't have any influence over Taggart, I'd just like to have your honest opinion.'

Tasha tried desperately to talk her way out of this, but Phil kept talking over her every time she made excuses. Looking into the anxious blue eyes, she suddenly realised why Chaz found it so appealing to take out his frustrations on the man. The way she felt now, she'd like nothing *better* than to go back with Phil and *encourage* him to try to seduce her just for the satisfaction of seeing him do himself out of one hundred thousand dollars. If she was miserable, why shouldn't everyone else be? But just because Chaz sank that low didn't mean she had to.

She raised a hand and hailed a cab. 'It was lovely, Phil,' she lied. 'But some other time.'

She got into the taxi and closed the door. Phil was still talking when the driver pulled out into traffic.

# CHAPTER TEN

TASHA'S taxi inched along through the traffic. She stared sombrely ahead. She was having to face something she should have recognised long ago. Chaz was not fundamentally different from the man she'd hated all those years. He was exasperating, cynical, ruthless; he was spectacularly talented, effortlessly attractive, and too clever not to know it and use both to his advantage. The only difference was that now she was in love with him. It hurt to see him with someone else; it hurt to see him *want* someone else.

Toni's career was taking off. She didn't have a lot of time, and she was—had to be—ruthless too. She wasn't going to wait around indefinitely for Chaz to be free. Which meant that all Tasha had to do to keep them apart was—nothing.

She could just let the marriage drift along for a year to the divorce they'd agreed on. And by the time it was over Toni would be gone, and Chaz's second chance would be gone. Even if Tasha couldn't have him herself she could keep someone else from having him, just as she'd already kept Toni away just by being married to Chaz and having the automatic right to be the woman who lived with him. Chaz wouldn't want to go on being married, of course. He'd probably go back to having a different woman every other week. But at least nobody else would have the real thing.

The old Tasha would have been far too decent and nice to even *consider* such a thing. But love did funny things to you. Toni had so much—whatever happened, she was going to have that wonderful talent, and thanks to Chaz she would have the recognition she deserved. Why should Tasha step aside, and take on not just a couple of minutes of that stabbing pain but a whole *lifetime* of it, just so Toni could have everything? All right, maybe it wouldn't be a lifetime of agony, maybe it would be just a couple of years—but it would be a lifetime of loneliness, since she'd certainly never find anyone to match Chaz. He wasn't the type of man you could rebound from, because there wouldn't be anyone to rebound to. Well, why *should* she make it any worse for herself?

She knew the answer as soon as she asked the question. The only way she could make it better for herself, in the horrible, selfish way that counted as better, was by making it worse for him. She'd take away something he cared about more than anything in the world. She *knew* how much he cared, and how much it would hurt him, because she knew how she felt. And she couldn't do it. She couldn't. She just couldn't.

Tasha had been rehearsing ways of breaking the news, but they all deserted her as soon as she walked in the door. She'd been half hoping Chaz would not be back, but he was stretched out on the sofa watching a video. Toni's voice prowled through a song like a lion cub with velvet paws; no wonder he was in love with her, Tasha thought bitterly.

Chaz sat up and switched off the video as she came through the door.

'She's amazing,' Tasha said stiffly. Her eyes were devouring him, as if she were seeing him for the last time—the clean line of his jaw, the curve of his mouth, the hook of his nose, oh, and those exasperating, sardonic eyebrows. The long, lean body, with its athlete's strength and grace. It was as if she were seeing them now for the first time—too late. She could not help thinking bitterly of all the opportunities she'd passed up for the casual, meaningless sex which was all he had to offer her, and which would at least have been something to look back on while Chaz found out, at last, what it was like to sleep with someone he loved. Well, too late now.

'Yes, she is,' he said. He was frowning.

Tasha looked into his face. He didn't look like someone tormented by lost love. He looked pretty much the way he always did. It would be so easy to let the moment pass. If she did she would probably never find the courage she needed again.

Right, well, it was time to put an end to it.

'Chaz,' said Tasha.

'Tasha,' he said mockingly.

'I—I don't really know how to say it,' she said, 'but I don't think this is working. I think we should get a divorce now and just go back to our own lives.'

'What exactly do you think isn't working?' he asked.

'The whole thing,' she said. 'I'm just treading water. I need to look for a job at a level where I can actually learn something and make a contribution. I can't take the kind of job your contacts would get me. I'll be ready for that in a few years, and I want it when I've earned it, not when I don't know what I'm doing. I just drift along with you, and I take up a lot of your time when you could be free for doing whatever you want to do.'

He was just watching her. She couldn't read his expression.

'I—I shouldn't really have accepted your offer in the first place,' she said. 'You got me out of a tight spot, but I don't *need* you to keep rescuing me for a whole year.'

'It's not much of a rescue to give you a place to stay,' he said. 'I'm sorry if I got in the way of job-hunting, but there's nothing to stop you if that's what you want to do.

You're not getting in the way of anything I want to do with my time if that's what's worrying you.'

It was as if all the charm had leached out of his voice, leaving only a dry, businesslike stranger. What could Toni have said to him? That she never wanted to see him again? Was it already too late for him?

'I just—' Tasha tried desperately to think of some other practical reason to start divorce proceedings *now*, and failed.

'Don't think it's working,' he said at last, when she stopped mid-sentence. 'All right. You don't have to justify yourself to me, Tasha.' He ran a hand through his hair. 'Do you want to stay here until you find something that suits you better?'

'If you don't mind.'

'Fine. I'll get onto my lawyer in the morning to draw up the papers.'

'Thank you.' Tasha stood staring down at him, her eyes still devouring him. He was in love with someone else, and he *knew* he was. But just supposing… Supposing you had a thousand to one chance of something to remember all your life, and all you had to do was something you'd be ashamed of all your life to get it?

'Er…' she said.

'Is there something else?' said Chaz, glancing up at her.

'I just wondered,' said Tasha.

'Wondered what?'

'You said if I ever changed my mind I could say,' she said. 'I wondered if you would like to spend a night together before I go.' It sounded like a card with RSVP in copperplate at the bottom corner, but at least it was said.

It was said, but for a moment she thought he hadn't understood her. He stared at her, and then he laughed. 'Natasha, darling,' he said, 'you do pick your moments, don't you?' He raised an eyebrow. 'If there ever was a time when that would have been a good idea, Tasha, don't you think it's long since gone?'

Her cheeks were hot, but she could feel her temper flare up. She was handing him his life on a plate, and all he could do was sneer. 'If I'd thought that I wouldn't have *said* it,' she snapped. 'You don't have to be horrible, Chaz. I was just *asking*.'

'Sorry,' he said with a shrug. 'Well, I just said no. Anything else?'

'*No,*' Tasha said grittily. 'Or rather, yes.' She looked at him through narrowed eyes. 'Phil *hasn't* made a pass at me,' she told him. 'So it looks as though you'll lose *that* particular bet.' He'd lose it if she had to lock herself into her room for a month.

'Could be,' he said indifferently. He stood up.

'Where are you going?' she asked.

'I've got a few people to see,' he said, not bothering to come up with a plausible pretext. 'I'll catch you later.'

He left the room without further comment. She didn't even have the satisfaction of stalking out and slamming a door.

Tasha spent the evening in her room trying to read. Then she tried to watch TV. Then she tried to listen to a CD. Nothing worked. Not only was she going to have to spend the rest of her life without Chaz, she was going to spend it with that horrible voice going through her mind saying 'Well, I just said no.'

She had to force herself to leave her room the next morning. She was going to have to eat some time; she couldn't just avoid Chaz until she moved out. But the smell of fresh coffee as she approached the kitchen almost made her turn back.

'Coffee?'

She hadn't thought she'd made any noise, but he must have heard her.

She gritted her teeth and walked through the kitchen door. 'Thanks,' she said, flashing a look at his face and then looking elsewhere before he could sneer.

He poured coffee into a mug, added milk and put it on the kitchen table in front of her.

'Thanks,' she said again, looking at the mug. She picked it up, holding it with her hands moulded round the body of the mug. The hot china scorched her palms, the hot liquid scalded her mouth, but she kept holding the mug and drinking, as if the fierce heat might dissolve the cold misery inside her.

Chaz had the paper open to the financial section. He went back to reading it, taking an occasional sip of coffee.

There was a plate of fresh bagels on the table. She would probably just go back to Britain and not even be able to get a decent bagel. Tasha stretched out a hand to take one and brought it to her mouth; she was about to take a bite when she realised that just the thought of chewing made her feel sick.

She put it on the table. She took another sip of coffee and then just stood there, cradling the mug in her hands.

'Tasha?' said Chaz.

'Yes?' she said.

'Look at me,' he said.

She raised her eyes. He wasn't sneering, anyway.

'Look, I'm sorry,' he said. 'I never meant to make you unhappy.'

'It doesn't matter,' she said. 'It's not your fault.'

Chaz raised an eyebrow. 'Of course it's my fault,' he said. 'It was my idea in the first place. You've every right to end it whenever you choose. You've every right to suggest we spend one last night together, if that's what you

want; I may not think it's a good idea, but that's no reason
to blow you out of the water.'

'It's all right,' said Tasha. She took a sip of the hot coffee
to keep her teeth from chattering.

'No, it's not all right,' said Chaz. He gave her a rather
wry smile. 'Look, Tash, you've known me a long time. You
know I've a filthy temper and the devil's own tongue and
I don't try as hard as I should to control it, but surely we
can do better than this? We got on all right for a while,
didn't we? Even if we do call it off, let's at least be friends.'

'All right,' said Tasha.

'Really all right? As in you'll let me take you out to
dinner tonight?'

She wouldn't be seeing much more of him. It was better
than nothing. 'All right,' she said again. 'I mean, yes, I'd
like that.'

'Then it's a deal. I'll book a table for eight o'clock.'

Chaz left for a meeting and Tasha spent the morning prowl-
ing around the apartment. Lunchtime came and went without lunch; she still felt as though eating would make her
sick. At last she decided to go for a walk. Anything to stop
looking at the walls.

She had reckoned without a forgotten adversary.

She had walked for perhaps a block when someone
called her name. She turned, and found Phil coming towards her with a look of pleased surprise.

'Tasha!' he exclaimed. 'What a lovely surprise.'

Tasha fenced with him unsuccessfully. Phil had not been
keeping a watch on the apartment just to be fobbed off by
someone who had other things on her mind.

Sure enough, Phil repeated his invitation to come and
see what he was working on. Reluctantly she accompanied
him to his sixth-floor apartment in an old brownstone.

The apartment was in chaos. There were papers and dirt

lishes scattered everywhere, and the bed she glimpsed through one half-open door was unmade. Phil seemed rather proud of the disorder, as if he were introducing her to a glamorous Bohemian existence.

He managed to assemble a few sheets of paper with sketches and outlines of the book, but it all seemed so neb-lous that Tasha was surprised he'd thought it worth bring-ing her back to show her. What she saw she didn't like, but after all the book was only in its preliminary stages.

Finally she said, 'I really must go. Thank you for show-ing me this.'

Phil gave her an intimate smile. 'Don't go, Tasha. We've only just started to get to know each other.' And to her astonishment he threw his arms around her and kissed her wetly on the mouth.

Tasha jerked away.

'I'm sorry,' he said. 'I know it's too soon—by conven-tional standards.' The blue eyes glowed. 'We haven't known each other very long. There are all kinds of things we don't know about each other. But when the chemistry is there you always know.'

Well, thought Tasha, you could certainly tell when the chemistry *wasn't* there. She supposed it would be rude to wipe off her mouth. She said, 'I'm afraid I just thought we were going to look at the book, Phil.'

Phil gave her a knowing smile. 'I think we both know why you came here,' he said. 'Let's not pretend.'

'I'm not pretending,' Tasha said indignantly.

'I think I know you better than you know yourself,' said Phil. 'Please, Tasha, let's be honest.' The blue eyes were guileless. 'You're the most wonderful woman I've met in years,' he said. 'I knew the first moment I saw you that you would be important to me. I know I shouldn't say this now, but I'm going to say it anyway—I'd like to sleep with you, and I think you'd like to sleep with me too. Can't you throw off your inhibitions and admit that? I can't think of a more wonderful way to spend the afternoon than going to my bedroom and getting to know you better.'

Tasha glared at him. She could think of a much nicer way of spending the afternoon. She could start off by telling him about the three hundred thousand dollars he'd just thrown away by being an inconsiderate, conceited, selfish toad, and then go back to her own apartment and make wild, passionate love to her husband. Except, of course, that she wasn't going to make wild, passionate love to her husband ever again. Well, if she couldn't sleep with Chaz she *certainly* didn't want to sleep with this idiot.

'I'm sorry, Phil,' she said crisply. 'I'm afraid I completely misunderstood what you had in mind. I'm sorry I can't help you, but I simply don't have the kind of influence that could help you with Chaz.'

Phil looked at her sullenly. 'What you mean is you don't *want* to help,' he said accusingly. 'Anyone can see he's crazy about you.'

This was the first interesting thing he'd said all afternoon.

'What?' said Tasha.

'When I heard he'd married I couldn't imagine who'd be clever enough to catch him,' he said. 'I couldn't believe it till I saw it. His eyes were following you around the room. If you wanted to ask for it you could get a damned sight more than a lousy sixty thousand dollars.'

'I really don't think—' began Tasha.

'When Taggart got back from Europe with you he was like a different man. As it turns out, it may not have mattered in the long run, but at the time it looked as if he'd thrown away five years' preparation…'

'Phil,' said Tasha, 'I haven't the faintest idea of what you're talking about, but I can *assure* you that you're making some kind of mistake.'

'Oh *really*?' sneered Phil. 'Look, how much do you know about the WQBQ deal?'

'He decided it wasn't for him,' said Tasha. 'He never said why.'

'WQBQ,' said Phil, 'was one of a kind. Taggart has had his eye on it ever since he came over here; everyone knows that. Every so often he'd meet the owners just to show what a great guy he was, how he understood the philosophy, wouldn't change the character... About six months ago he heard they were beginning to think seriously about selling. He sold off his production company so he could move fast when the time came. Finally the time comes to talk turkey; the owners are actually going to give him first refusal. Only he's over in England. At first he says it's just for a couple of days. Then he says no, he's getting married and then he's going on a honeymoon.'

'How do you know all this?' asked Tasha.

'*Everyone* knows it,' said Phil. 'Jack Vale was going insane. He kept calling people he thought could get Taggart to listen to reason, except Taggart had *turned off his cell-phone*.'

Tasha stifled a hysterical giggle.

'Well, the owners were furious,' Phil went on. 'They said they'd just sell to the highest bidder, but they couldn't quite face it—wanted to give him a second chance—Vale managed to track him down to his hotel. No, he's enjoying his honeymoon, thanks but no thanks.' He looked at her resentfully. 'You can't tell *me* he's not wild for you,' he said. 'You can't tell *me* he wouldn't do anything you asked me to.'

He attempted a look of shamefaced and disarming contrition, and failed. 'I'm sorry about just now,' he said. 'My feelings overcame my better judgement. I suppose it wasn't very chivalrous of me to bring you back here under false pretences. My only excuse is I don't often meet someone who has such a powerful impact on—'

Tasha stared at him. 'It wasn't very what?' she said.

'Chivalrous. But as I say—'

'Phil,' said Tasha, breaking in ruthlessly, 'I can't stay any longer. I need to think about this.'

# CHAPTER ELEVEN

SEVERAL hours went by. It was now late afternoon. A brilliant blue sky was above her; the street was in shadow. Tasha walked along, frowning; she was trying to take in a possibility so absolutely unbelievable…

Again and again the memory of a cold, rainy night came back to her; how she'd stumbled into the house and found only Chaz; how he'd kissed her. 'In case you hadn't noticed I'm being chivalrous for the first time in my life.' Didn't that mean it had been the first time he hadn't wanted to rush someone? But in that case didn't that mean the vulnerable street girl who'd captured his heart was just as much a figment of her imagination as the innocent girl with traditional values? That the girl Chaz had thought was right for him was—?

But that was just impossible. How could Chaz be in love with her? All he ever did was tease her. He'd been horrible to her for years. Phil had said he was crazy about her—but poor, self-obsessed, deluded Phil would naturally see only what made it likelier for him to get what he wanted.

But Chaz had *said* it was the first time he'd been chivalrous. Of course, it was just conceivable that Tasha had been the girl he had in mind, and he'd then come across Toni in Paris and fallen in love with her. But then almost everything she'd read into his relationship with Toni had been based on the assumption that Toni was the girl.

The fact was, she realised, that she herself wanted so desperately to believe she'd been wrong that she had lost all sense for what was likely.

The only way to find out, she thought, gritting her teeth,

was to ask him. It had been bad enough to ask him to sleep with her and be rejected. What would it be like to ask if he was in love with her? She could just imagine his eyes widening in astonishment, the eyebrow raised at someone who just couldn't take no for an answer. Men with not even a particle of his talent and charisma had walked out on her, and she thought Chaz, of all impossible people, might have fallen in love with her instead.

It sounded preposterous. But then Phil had said—

She ended up walking the streets for six hours. It was long past dark by the time she got home.

She walked into the flat to find Chaz in the front room pacing up and down, a drink in his hand.

'Where the hell have you been?' he asked. He looked furious, but at least he was there, and he wasn't giving her the cold shoulder.

'Oh, just walking,' said Tasha vaguely. 'I ran into Phil.' She glanced at her watch. 'Oh, is that the time?' she said still vaguely. 'I wasn't really paying attention...'

Chaz made an obvious effort to control his temper.

'Well, tell me all,' he said. 'Has he decided the fate of cheque number three, or is the verdict still out?'

'No, you can tear it up,' Tasha said distractedly. 'He said he knew it was too soon by conventional standards but he was going to ask me anyway, so he asked me, so it looks as though you were right.'

'Well, you could at least have the decency to mind losing,' said Chaz. 'You've taken all the fun out of it.'

Tasha stared at him. He didn't *look* as though he was crazy about her. On the other hand...

If she asked him chances were he'd throw back his head and howl with laughter. But...

'What is it, Tasha?' asked Chaz. 'Did he upset you, darling? Do you want me to give him a bloody nose and two black eyes?'

Tasha shook her head. 'No,' she said slowly. 'He didn't upset me. He was a terrible bore, but he did say one thing that was quite…interesting.'

'Which was?' said Chaz. 'Come on, Tash, you can't stop now. The suspense is killing me.' An amused smile pulled at his mouth.

Right, thought Tasha. It was now or never.

'Chaz,' she said.

'Yes, Tasha?' said Chaz.

'Could I ask you a question?'

'I don't like the sound of this,' said Chaz. 'But fire away.'

Tasha steeled herself. 'You remember that night when I told you the wedding was off?' she said.

'Vividly,' said Chaz. 'What about it?'

'You said you were being chivalrous for the first time in your life,' said Tasha. 'Was that true?'

Suddenly he was very still.

'Yes.'

'And you said you didn't want to rush the girl you thought was the right one for you,' she said.

'Yes.'

'So that was—you thought that was me?' said Tasha, believing it less and less as she spoke the words.

'I'm afraid so.'

She had to ask it. 'Not Toni?' she said.

'*Toni?*' He didn't exactly howl with laughter, but the sardonic eyebrow she'd been dreading shot up at the suggestion.

Tasha stared at him. 'You're in love with me?' she said.

'For my sins.' He gave her a quizzical glance. 'Is all this courtesy of Mr Jones?'

'He said you were crazy about me,' said Tasha.

'It's one way of putting it.'

'But how can you possibly be in love with me?' she said. 'You've always been horrible to me.'

'Self-defence, probably.' He shrugged.

'You're always laughing at me.'

'You make me laugh. It's one of the things I like about you.'

She'd thought if her long shot was right she'd be ecstatic, but in fact she was afraid to believe it. She could have walked straight into his arms, but she just stood staring at his face, trying to *see* in the features that looked exactly the same some sign that it was really true.

Chaz laughed wryly. 'Come and sit down, Tash,' he said. 'I'll pour you a good stiff drink and tell you all about it.'

'I'd better not have anything to drink,' she said. 'I haven't eaten for quite a while.'

'Then come into the kitchen and you can eat while I talk.'

Tasha followed him into the kitchen and sank wearily onto one of the tall wooden stools that surrounded the central counter.

'I think I won't eat after all,' she said. 'I'm too tired.'

Chaz put a stick of French bread on the cutting board, and began taking things out of the fridge: ten kinds of cheese, five kinds of pâté, three kinds of olives, jars of caviare and sun-dried tomatoes and artichoke hearts.

'I'm really not hungry,' Tasha protested.

'Sure you are,' he said. 'I'll open a bottle of wine while you get started.'

He took a bottle of red from a rack, opened it and left it to breathe on the counter. Then he sat down on a stool across the counter from her.

He said, 'I don't know if you remember, or ever knew, but at one point your father as good as told me not to come back to the house. I was in my first year at university; I'd had to come by train because I'd run my car off the road after a party, and I made some kind of joke about it.' He shrugged. 'It was the only time I've seen him really angry—he started talking in this very cold, hyper-logical way about drinking and driving.' He flicked up an eyebrow. 'I don't know if he was hoping for a manly admission of error; as you can imagine, I didn't take it with a very good grace. Finally he asked if I would kill a child to get to a party and I said I thought it would depend on the child and the party.'

He grinned mirthlessly. 'He wasn't exactly amused. He said he'd like the key to his house back, and he said he thought it would be better if I spent my vacations at one of the many houses where I would no doubt be welcome. I went off in a huff and didn't come back for a couple of years. Then one weekend I went to a house party and it was bloody awful. I remember looking around at midnight and thinking how ghastly it would be to see all these people the next day, and I thought if I just left I could turn up at your father's for breakfast. I waited till I'd sobered up, but I still got there at five, too early to wake people up and of course I didn't have a key, so I just sat at the bottom of the drive, looking out over the water meadows.'

He frowned, remembering. 'Gradually the sky started to lighten. The moon was still in the sky, not washed out and pale the way you sometimes see it but this huge bright silver disc just above the horizon. Then the sun started to come up. I've never seen such a colour; it was like a ball of molten gold coming through the trees. It was still very low, of course; where the grass lay open to the sun it was tipped with gold, but where the sun was blocked off by a wall or a tree the grass was still that ghostly silver from the light of the moon.

'After a while I saw someone coming through the grass. At first all I could see was hair like the sun, paler but with that same burning intensity. Then something, perhaps a

wall, cut off the sun, and in the bluish light all I could see
was hair the bright silver of the moon. She kept coming,
and whatever light there was her hair threw it off in silver
or gold...There must have been a path through the grass
but I couldn't see it; suddenly she came up out of the field
onto the road. It was bloody cold, but her feet were bare.
She came right up to me and we looked at each other. Her
eyes were huge, this deep, misty green, and she kept staring
at me and I kept staring back. Then she just walked off
without a word.'

Chaz looked at Tasha. 'You're not eating,' he said.
'Come on, Tash, you'll feel better when you've had something.'

Tasha broke off a piece of bread and put some cheese
on it.

'I keep saying she when of course it was you,' he said.
'But at the time it was all so strange I didn't realise it. I
suppose it was partly the fact that she'd—you'd—looked
straight in my face without recognising me.'

'I used to sleepwalk when I was younger,' said Tasha.

'Well, that must have been it. Anyway, as you probably
know I was reading English when I could spare time for it
between parties, which wasn't often. It reminded me of
something I was supposed to have written an essay on,
though in fact I think I'd charmed my tutor into letting me
off. ''I met a lady in the meads Full beautiful, a faery's
child; Her hair was long, her foot was light, And her eyes
were wild.'' It kept going through my head anyway; I kept
seeing this girl come up to me out of the mist, barefoot,
with those wild green eyes.'

He cut several slices of bread and put them on her plate,
and began cutting sections of cheese and putting them on
the plate too until she waved his hand away.

'Well, fast forward a couple of hours. I went up to the
house; your father welcomed me back to the fold; I went

into breakfast, and there she—you—were. I recognised you now, of course, and you recognised me, and were obviously just as delighted to see me as you'd always been.' He gave her a wry smile. 'You had a lot of presents in front of you, and your father explained that it was your sixteenth birthday.'

Tasha was on the point of taking a bite of bread and cheese in her mouth, but at this she put it down again. 'My sixteenth birthday?' she said. 'But Chaz, I remember *perfectly* well—'

He grinned. 'I was afraid of that. Mind if I go on?'

She shook her head.

'I don't know if you've ever seen the film *Roman Holiday*? Audrey Hepburn plays a princess who slips the leash for a day in Rome, rides around on a Vespa with cynical journo hack Gregory Peck?' An eyebrow flicked up. 'It was kind of like that. You still looked like something on a visit from another planet; it was as if you were saying, "What do ordinary people wear here? Oh, jeans and a T-shirt! Well, when in Rome..." You were wearing jeans and a T-shirt and opening all these poxy presents and looking thrilled every time someone gave you a bottle of cheap eau-de-Cologne, and all the time you still had hair like a scary sun and those wild, wild eyes.'

He shrugged ruefully. 'Anyway, people went their ways after breakfast and you started folding up the wrapping paper and I thought I'd better say something. So I went up and said something kind of offhand and joky, the kind of thing I'd have said to one of the girls in my set, and you just stood up and walked off without a word.'

'*Yes,*' said Tasha. 'Because you'd just turned up out of the blue and *ruined* my sixteenth birthday.' She glared at him. 'You came up to me and said, "How does it feel to have reached the age of consent?" And I said, "What?"'

And you said, "Can I be the first in line now that it's legal?" How *could* you, Chaz?'

He groaned. 'I was hoping you'd forgotten.'

'How could I *ever* forget something like that?' said Tasha. 'And if you really thought you'd fallen in love why would you gratuitously insult me?'

He smiled wryly. 'I was nervous.'

Tasha gave him a sceptical look. Chaz picked up the bottle of wine and filled two glasses.

'Anyway, it wasn't meant as an insult, Tash,' he said. 'I kept telling myself you were just sixteen; sixteen-year-olds always like to pretend to be sexually experienced even if they're not, they like to be treated as more sophisticated than they are. I thought you'd be flattered if someone who was almost twenty-one talked to you the way he'd talk to girls his own age. It was a joke. It just kind of came out wrong.'

'And I suppose you didn't mean to insult Michael, either,' said Tasha.

'Of course I meant to insult him,' Chaz said. 'He was a complete prat and he had the nerve to think he was your boyfriend. I couldn't believe my eyes when he showed up for lunch.'

Tasha sipped her wine, looking at him seriously over the rim. 'But how can you—? I mean, if you think you've been in love with me all that time, how could you—?' She couldn't begin to sum up all the ways Chaz had behaved abominably over the years.

He shrugged. 'Well, you always made it so clear you didn't like me that there was obviously no point in just coming out and saying it. And every time I came back you always had some disgusting barnacle of a boyfriend attached, which did tend to bring out the worst in me.' He smiled. 'But that night at your father's, as soon as I kissed you everything was all right. I might always *say* the wrong thing, but on some other level it was all right. I thought I couldn't let this slip, if I waited you'd just find some other revolting boyfriend, whereas if we were actually married and spent some time together at least there'd be a *chance*. And I thought if we had a physical relationship it would be obvious to you how I felt even if I always said the wrong things.'

He grimaced. 'It hadn't occurred to me you'd put it all down to technique, or that you'd just see your own response as some kind of physical reflex. I didn't really know what to do after that. I thought if we went on having good sex you'd just go on thinking it was all expertise, so I tried to back off, and that didn't seem to work either. And then you said you wanted a divorce, so that was that.'

'I only said it because I thought you were in love with Toni,' said Tasha. 'I thought she was the girl you told me about. I thought I was standing in your way and that you'd never have another chance.'

He frowned, looking back. 'Oh, I see.'

'I saw the way she kissed you when she left, and she said something in French, and after she left you were so remote.'

'What she said was that you can seduce the body but not the heart,' he said. 'She said ''Now you know what it feels like to be kissed by someone who can make your body say yes when your heart says no. Now every time you kiss her you'll know how she feels. If you want to know how she feels in your bed you can spend a night in mine.'''

Tasha stared at him open-mouthed. 'She said *that*? After all you'd done for her?'

Chaz laughed. 'Well, she was never one for pulling her punches. You should be cheering.'

'What did you say?' she asked.

He raised an eyebrow. 'Well, if I'd really wanted to twist

the knife I'd have said something nice about her technique, but I think I just said I knew how she felt.'

He said, 'The thing is, I like being with you; it doesn't really matter what we're doing. We could be watching re-runs of snooker semi-finals and I wouldn't be bored, because you were there. I kept thinking the time would come when I could just say it. I love you and I want you to be my wife.'

'I am your wife,' said Tasha.

'My permanent wife,' said Chaz. He gave her a gleaming glance. 'The kind you have children with to look at your wedding album.'

'So we don't have to get divorced after all,' she joked.

'Don't we?'

*'What?'*

Chaz slid his wedding ring off his finger. 'Give me yours,' he said.

She slipped the gold band off and handed it to him.

'I want a divorce as soon as it's humanly possible to get one,' he said calmly.

'But—' said Tasha.

'And I'd like you to move into a place of your own.'

'But—' said Tasha.

'And then,' he said coolly, 'when it's absolutely clear that I've no claims on you of any kind, I'll ask you to marry me again.'

*'What?'* said Tasha.

'If you decide, as a completely free agent, that you can love someone who, as you've told me over the years, is devious, cynical, manipulative and completely untrustworthy, but who also happens to think life isn't worth living without you, then we'll put on these rings again. If not we shouldn't be wearing them.'

Tasha wondered, for a moment, whether Chaz had gone quietly insane while she hadn't been looking.

'I tricked you into marrying me,' he said. 'I tricked you into sleeping with me. I thought it didn't matter *how* we got together because once we did you'd see, deep down, that we belonged together.' His black eyes were hard. 'I can't say I wish I hadn't done it, because if I hadn't I'd have lost you. But I did something terrible in bringing you into that kind of marriage, and it's time it was undone.'

Tasha struggled to put a stop to this lunacy. 'Well, it *was* devious, manipulative and untrustworthy,' she said. Maybe if she made a joke of it he'd come to his senses. 'And cynical, too, but if I'm not worried about that I don't see why you should be.'

She might as well not have spoken. He didn't even crack a smile. 'You don't understand,' he said. 'I flew over to talk to your father on the off-chance that something could kill the wedding—insane, of course, but I knew he was none too keen on Jeremy.' He frowned, looking back. 'Out of the blue, I'm handed on a plate a chance to have you to myself. It may not be much of a chance, but I'm never going to see a better. It means kissing WQBQ goodbye—*probably*, but not certainly, because there's a fair chance the owners will get cold feet. Whereas if I try to keep the deal alive I'll almost *certainly* never be in the same room with you again for longer than it takes you to make up a polite excuse to leave it.'

Tasha would have liked to make a polite demur, but she had to admit this was a fair description of her attitude to Chaz up to a few months ago. 'Well?' she said.

'It didn't take me two seconds to weigh up the odds. If I went through with it there was no way I couldn't come out ahead—because *whatever* happened I had a year with you guaranteed. If the gamble paid off I'd have you for the rest of my life; if it didn't, at least I'd have had the year.'

Tasha wished he didn't look so grim. You'd have

thought he was confessing to a crime instead of telling her he'd have done anything to be with her.

'As soon as we got married I knew I was right,' he said. 'Not about getting you to fall in love with me, God knows, but just spending all that time with you whether you wanted to or not. Whatever happens you can't take that away from me. I'll always be able to look back and remember how lovely you were.' He smiled at her. 'You asked me once if it was any different sleeping with someone you love and I didn't know the answer. Now I know the answer. You can't take that away from me either. I got more than I'd any right to expect, and it didn't seem absolutely impossible that I might win out in the end.'

He ran a hand impatiently back through his hair. 'I didn't think about what I was doing to you. I know what you're afraid of, and I kept thinking you'd come to trust me and I could tell you you didn't have to be afraid any more, and it never occurred to me that—'

'What I'm *afraid* of?' Tasha interrupted.

'You're afraid of things that don't last,' he said. 'You look at me and think you see the personification of everything you hate. Here today and gone tomorrow. Permanently provisional. I think...' He hesitated, then shrugged and went on, 'I think you're attracted to me on more levels than the physical, but the things that attract you attract a lot of other people too. You don't want to be in competition. You're afraid if you let yourself respond to something you find obviously attractive someone else will take it away from you.'

He grimaced. 'I thought I could convince you that you didn't have to be afraid of that. I'd been trying for years to forget about you; for better or worse I was yours. I thought sooner or later you'd see that. But how could you when I'd brought you into a marriage based on a lie? I wanted you to trust your instincts and all I ever did was tempt you to go against them. I wanted you to see I couldn't look at anyone else—but after all I'd pretended I was only casually interested in you; why on earth *shouldn't* you think I'd go off with anyone else who happened to attract me?'

Tasha had the feeling that she was being inexorably swept along by arguments that made no sense. Perhaps she could take refuge in the law.

'Are people *allowed* to do that?' she asked. 'Get divorced and then turn around and get married again the same day?'

'I don't know,' he shrugged. 'Probably depends on the state.'

'Would we have to invite everybody again?'

Chaz smiled faintly. 'Natasha, darling, we can do anything you want. It can be a private ceremony for just the two of us; we can hand out invitations to the first five thousand callers to WQBQ; or we can invite everyone who enjoyed Wedding to join us for Wedding II. But aren't you taking a lot for granted? What are the odds that you'll say yes the second time around? The first time it was the lesser of two evils, the greater evil being cancellation of one of the most diabolically elaborate weddings I've ever seen. Next time you'll have to think the only thing worse than living with me is living without me. Can't see it happening myself.'

He was still holding the two rings in his hand. He looked down at them, then shrugged and dropped them in a black lacquer bowl on the table.

'I'll see you in the morning,' he said.

# CHAPTER TWELVE

TASHA sat on her stool, legs curled up beneath her, staring at the two gold rings in the gleaming black bowl. How had this happened? Why couldn't he just kiss her again? Why couldn't he just say he'd like to know what it was like to sleep with someone he loved who loved him too? He could say it with that lurking smile in his eyes, because he always knew what to say and how to say it. Why was she sitting on a sofa alone instead of standing in his bedroom taking off his clothes making up for all the lost time?

What was wrong with him, anyway? First he said she should marry him but it wouldn't mean a thing. Now he said he couldn't live without her and he wanted a divorce. He'd explained for something like two hours and the more he'd gone on explaining the less anything had made sense.

'Next time you'll have to think the only thing worse than living with me is living without me.' But she *already* thought that. Why couldn't he see that? 'I thought...you'd see, deep down, that we belonged together.' Why couldn't he see that she loved being with him? It wasn't *her* fault that she'd had to stand around watching him trade jokes in French with the hottest new singer in New York—how was she *supposed* to know he didn't think, deep down, that he belonged with someone else?

She'd been sitting there for a couple of hours when something occurred to her. Chaz had done practically all the talking. She'd come back and asked a question and he'd answered it. Then she'd asked some more questions and he'd answered them. She'd hardly said anything at all.

It wasn't exactly her fault—after all, he'd hardly give

ner a chance to get a word in. But what *had* she actually
said? 'So we don't have to get divorced after all.' Was that
it?

She ran her mind back over the conversation. Obviously
he must have said 'I love you too' at some stage. Or if
he hadn't said it in so many words it must have been
obvious…

But if what he'd said was true, he'd been in love with
her for years knowing she could hardly stand to be in the
same room with him. As far as he knew, she'd thought he
was in love with Toni and offered him a divorce without a
fight. No wonder he didn't think she'd want to go through
with it again if she had the choice.

Tasha scowled. The sentence 'I love you too' might have
been missing from the conversation, but so had 'How do
you feel about it?' and 'What do you think?' and 'What
would you like to do?' On the other hand, what could you
expect from someone who'd always succeeded at everything he set out to do? He was used to ordering people
round; he was used to making decisions without consulting anyone. Motto: when in doubt, be decisive.

Well, he'd just said no again, but that didn't mean she
had to take it for an answer.

Suddenly, with a shrug, she snatched up the two gleaming bands and walked back down the hall to his bedroom.
It was empty. So was the bathroom.

Motto two was probably: when in doubt, work. Tasha
tried his office.

Chaz was sitting at his computer answering e-mails. He
swung round in his chair when he heard her come in; she
saw that he looked tired and drawn.

'Chaz,' she said.

'Yes?'

'I'd like you to put this back on,' she said in a rush,
holding out her hand.

He looked down at the two rings cupped in her hand bu made no move to take one. 'I'm glad you think that, and hope you still think so in a few months' time,' he said. 'Bu I meant what I said.'

'And nothing I can say will change your mind?'

'No.'

Tasha raised an eyebrow. 'What if I said I could neve marry a man who had divorced his first wife without con sulting her?'

Chaz opened his mouth. She put her hand over it. 'Talk ing for two hours is not consulting me,' she said sternly. had something important to say and you never gave me th chance.'

She could feel his lips forming the word 'what' unde her hand.

'I love you,' she said simply. 'You didn't let me say even once, and I'd have said it twenty times if you hadn had so many decisions to make.'

He seemed to be saying 'but'.

'I saw Toni walk out on you at the restaurant and thought you were about to lose your last chance with he I thought it would kill me to let her have you when she ha so much. She has that marvellous talent; why should sh have you too? And all I'd have to do to keep you apa was stick to our deal and go on living with you. But I ju couldn't do that to you. I thought I *had* to give you yo freedom.'

She dropped her hand. 'You said I'd have to think livin with you was better than living without you. I can't imagi living without you. I don't want to have to spend mont in some other apartment making dates to see you. I thir we should just go on the way we are now.'

This would have been an ideal moment for Chaz sweep her into his arms, but he just kept looking at h steadily. 'You say that now,' he said. 'But it's too importa for that. You can't spend the rest of your life in a marriage you were tricked into. If you still think you want to live with me when the divorce comes through we'll get married again and start off on the right foot.'

Tasha gritted her teeth. Well, she couldn't say she hadn't known what she was getting into. She already knew Chaz was infuriating. 'Chaz,' she said sweetly. 'You always say you'll do anything to make me happy. As soon as I tell you what I want you tell me you know it wouldn't make me happy. Are you *ever* going to take my word for what will make me happy, or are you going to go on making up my mind for me?'

'Of course I—' he began.

'WQBQ,' said Tasha without even pausing, 'has lost something like two-thirds of its advertisers since it changed hands. Every time another one jumps ship Jack Vale calls to complain about what might have been. Now he tells me the new owners want to sell. Are we going to do something interesting, like run a radio station, or do I have to look for some job I don't want so I can be completely independent when I say yes?'

'Of course if you—' he began.

'I want you to be my husband,' said Tasha. 'In fact, you actually *are* my husband. Are you seriously telling me that you're going to go ahead and file for divorce anyway? Are you telling me I'm going to have to contest this divorce because you want to marry me twice and I thought once was enough?'

'Well, I—'

'Give me your hand,' said Tasha.

He raised an eyebrow.

'And don't you dare give me the wrong one,' she added.

She took his hand in hers. 'You said one day I'd say all those things and mean them,' she said. 'You meant them the first time, but I didn't. Even if we don't have another

ceremony, you should hear me say them and mean them.
Her grey-green eyes held his steadily. 'I Natasha Susan
Merrill Taggart,' she began with a smile, 'take thee Chase
Adam Zachary Taggart…' She went through the vows
she'd repeated parrot-like at the wedding. '…until death us
do part,' she ended, and she slid the gold band back on the
finger where she had placed it four months before. Then
she turned his hand over and placed her own ring in the
palm.

He took her hand. 'I may have meant all those things,'
he said, 'but *you* didn't know I meant them. You thought
the only reason I could stand to go through with it was
because it was just a charade. You should hear me say them
and know I mean every word of it.' He smiled at her. '
Chase Adam Zachary Taggart take thee Natasha Susan
Merrill Taggart…' He went through the vows and slid the
ring back on her finger.

'And now,' said Chaz, 'you could do me a big favour.'

'What's that?' said Tasha.

He flicked up an eyebrow. 'Let me kiss you without go
ing in terror of another of your compliments on my mar
vellous technique.'

Tasha smiled. 'All right,' she said.

'Natasha,' he said softly, tracing one of the flyaway eye
brows with his thumb. 'La Belle Dame Sans Merci,' he
added, with a mocking smile. 'You are, damn you.' He
brushed her mouth with his.

'"Feelings have nothing to do with it",' he quoted, and
he kissed her fleetingly again.

'"Just a physical thing—"' And then his mouth was on
hers.

A long time later Tasha drew her head away. 'Oh, Chaz,'
she said.

'Don't you dare tell me it was wonderful,' he said. 'O
lovely. *Or* nice.'

'I wasn't going to say any of those things,' she said. She gave him a mocking smile, the sort of smile a fairy princess gives a mortal who has been insane enough to take her home. 'What I was *going* to say,' she said, 'was I think your technique is slipping.' Her silver-green eyes were mocking him too. 'You're obviously out of practice.'

He smiled at her. She was wearing jeans and a T-shirt, just as she had all those years ago; the light on her hair was not the light of a sun up too soon or a moon out too late, just the light of an ordinary desk-lamp. She still made all those ordinary things look strange. But she had put her hands on his shoulders; she was smiling at him as if to say he would stay in this ordinary world since he was there. 'I'll try again,' he said, and he kissed her again.

Tasha closed her eyes. His technique was really marvellous. It was wonderful. It was nice. It was really, really, really, really lovely.

A long time later she opened her eyes. Bad Cousin Chaz was smiling at her.

'How was that?' he said.

Tasha looked at him seriously.

'I hate to say this,' she said. 'But I think you're really going to have to work at it.'

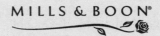

# Makes
## any time
## special

**Enjoy a romantic novel from**
*Mills & Boon*®

*Presents...*™    *Enchanted*™    *Temptation*®

*Historical Romance*™    *Medical Romance*™